A MISSISSIPPI SUNSET

Women of Courage Series
Book 3

A Novella

By Linda Weaver Clarke

Copyright © Linda Weaver Clarke, 2021. All rights reserved. No part of this book may be reproduced or transmitted in any form without permission in writing from the author. Recording of this work for the disability is permitted.

Red Mountain Shadows Publishing
Cover Design by Serena Clarke
Printed in the United States of America

A Mississippi Sunset
By Linda Weaver Clarke
www.lindaweaverclarke.com

ISBN: 9798418883308

Names, characters, places, and incidents are the product of the author's imagination, and any resemblance to actual persons, living or dead, events, or locales is purely coincidental.

BOOKS BY LINDA WEAVER CLARKE

**Women of Courage Series
(Historical Romance)**
*The Light at the End of the Tunnel
A Lady of Refinement
A Mississippi Sunset*

**Willow Valley Series
(Historical Mystery Romance)**
*One Last Dance
Angel's Serenade
A Pleasant Rivalry
Holidays in Willow Valley
Tales of Willow Valley*

**The Rebel Series
(Swashbuckling Romance)**
*The Rebels of Cordovia
The Highwayman of Cordovia
The Fox of Cordovia*

**Bear Lake Family Saga
(Historical Romance)**
*Melinda and the Wild West
Edith and the Mysterious Stranger
Jenny's Dream*

Sarah's Special Gift
Elena, Woman of Courage

The Adventures of John and Julia Evans (Mystery/Suspense)
Anasazi Intrigue
Mayan Intrigue
Montezuma Intrigue
Desert Intrigue
Intriguing Escapades

Amelia Moore Detective Series (Romantic Cozy Mysteries)
The Bali Mystery
The Shamrock Case
The Missing Heir
The Mysterious Doll
Her Lost Love
Mystery on the Bayou
The Lighthouse Secret

Biographies & Other Books
Bedtime Stories: Shadows In My Room
Searching for True Happiness
Reflections of the Heart
Never Too Late To Dream: Autobiography
Take A Walk With Marcus Weaver and Milred Gough: Biography
Collection of Biographies: Gilbert D. Weaver and Olive Clark Heritage
Collection of Biographies: John Gough and Melinda Robinson Heritage

Dedication

I dedicate this book to my great grandmother, Martha Raymer Weaver, who stood up against prejudice and injustice. She wasn't swayed when threatened by a mob. She held her head high and challenged them. She believed in women's rights and was against slavery. She was a strong courageous woman.

Chapter 1
1844

Laura McBride rose from her flowerbed and dusted off the dirt from her hands. Standing in front of her daisies, she stared down at their sweet little faces. "You have rights," she said firmly. "Stand up for what you believe!"

As she gazed down at her audience, Laura laughed to herself when she realized that she was rehearsing her speech to her flowers. But there was no better audience. Laura needed to practice and there was no better time than the present.

She marched to the end of the flowerbed and pointed to a daisy as she continued. "You! Do you enjoy music?" When the daisy nodded with the breeze, Laura smiled. "Then do something about it. Develop your talents. Sing praises to the heavens. You must believe in yourself. Every one of you has a talent that you can share with others. Let it shine forth! Don't hide it."

When she heard a deep chuckle from the road, Laura turned around and saw Deputy Davies sitting astride his horse and watching her. He was a handsome fellow with the darkest eyes she had ever seen in a man. She had noticed him several times in town but hadn't had the opportunity to be introduced. In passing, he would nod and give her a friendly smile. She liked his smile. Each time his eyes would light up, just like they were doing at that moment.

With humor in her voice, Laura said, "They grow better when I talk to them."

The deputy seemed quite amused. He chuckled once again, waved to her, and went on his way.

Most women would be embarrassed but not Laura. She was used to being in the public's eye. Turning back to her audience, she tried to concentrate as she pointed to a daisy. The pretty little flower seemed to nod as if realizing Laura was about to give her some sound advice.

"You need to fight for your rights. It is very important to let your opinions be known."

Laura frowned. Was she coming over too strong? Should she tone her speech down a little? If she did, would the women understand the importance of what she was telling them? She wanted them to stand up and be noticed, to get involved with civic affairs.

Furrowing her brow, she said firmly, "Stick up for what you believe. God is on our side."

When the daisies nodded their agreement, she extended her hand toward her audience. Taking a deep breath, she continued.

"In the Gospel of Matthew, it says: Let your light shine before men, that they may see your good works. Don't hide your light under a bushel. Put it on a candlestick so you can be noticed." Tilting her head curiously, she asked, "Is it all right to quote scripture in my speech? It seems that more and more people are doing it these days, especially with all the revival meetings going on all over the place. People are eagerly seeking religion. So there shouldn't be anything wrong with quoting scripture in my lectures. Right?"

The daisies nodded their agreement.

With a curt nod, she smiled. "That's exactly how I feel, too."

When she spied something familiar, Laura lost her concentration. Stepping closer, she moved the leaves aside. Apparently, her neighbor's hens didn't know where their home was and kept meandering over to her property to lay their eggs. Gathering them into her apron, she headed to the Armstrong residence.

Laura gave a rap at the front door and waited. When Preacher Armstrong greeted her, she held her apron out and showed him what she had.

"Oh, for heavens sake!" he exclaimed. "Are my hens trespassing once again?"

She laughed. "Yes, sir." Handing the eggs over to her neighbor, Laura said, "I found them in the middle of my garden this time."

Armstrong acted surprised. "Thank you. Why didn't you just keep them? No one would have been the wiser."

"Because they were not my eggs. Your chickens just wandered over to my place and settled down in my yard."

With a shake of his head, Preacher Armstrong said, "I'm speechless. I've never known anyone to be so honest."

Laura gave a shrug and turned to leave.

"Wait a minute, Miss McBride. I would like to reward you. Would you like to keep some for all the work of gathering them?"

Laura shook her head. "It's not necessary. I was glad to do it."

"But I want to show my appreciation."

She smiled and replied, "I'm fine. Don't worry about it."

The preacher sighed. "Your parents would be proud of you. Honesty is a good attribute for a young lady. By the way, where are your parents? I've noticed you're home alone."

"They had to leave town for a few weeks to visit my uncle. He's ailing and not doing well. Father is worried about him."

"I'm so sorry. If you need anything while they're gone, let me know."

Laura nodded. "Thank you for the offer."

"I noticed that you were out weeding and talking to your flowers again," said Armstrong with humor in his voice. "I worry about you. I think you need to meet some nice young men your age. You need to socialize. I don't think it's healthy to be home so much. If you come to my Sunday sermons, you'll be able to meet some eligible bachelors."

Holding back her laughter, she said, "I'll think about it."

With that said, she headed home. It was true. The only times she went out and socialized was when she was giving a lecture at women's organizations – where men did not attend. She enjoyed going to parties and dance socials but hadn't attended any since she moved to Willow Valley. She was much too busy and hadn't found the time.

Laura was a beautiful young woman with rich dark brown hair and sky blue eyes. If she had a weakness, dancing would be it. She had learned the most popular steps while attending school. Her dance card was always full because she was so graceful. She seemed to glide across the floor with no effort. Laura missed attending the dance socials. Of all the activities for young women, dancing was on the top of her list.

Collapsing under a tree, she leaned against the trunk to rest. Gazing at the flowers, she smiled. Hopefully her audience would be as receptive to her speech as her daisies had been.

Laura's memory went back to the day she had told her parents about her plans. They were shocked and not sure what to think. Fighting for women's rights was a subject that was not readily accepted. She remembered their conversation.

After confiding in her parents, her father exclaimed with a shake of his head, "You're wasting your time, young lady. It will never happen. There is too much opposition."

"You're getting your hopes up," her mother added. "I don't see how you can make a difference. You are only one person."

"All it takes is one person," Laura said with conviction. "If I can influence a hundred women, and if those women can influence another hundred and so forth, look at the outcome."

"I'm not sure if you know what you're getting yourself into, young lady," her father said with a frown.

Wanting to convince her parents that she was going to do some good in the world, Laura continued. "After meeting Elizabeth Stanton at Troy Seminary, I learned that she was fighting for women's rights and I wanted to be part of it."

Her father cocked his head curiously and said, "I haven't heard of her."

Laura grinned and said with confidence, "You will. Trust me! You will."

"I don't understand why you're so adamant about this subject," he said with bewilderment. "This was not the reason we sent you to Troy Seminary. We had hoped to give you an education. We had hoped that you would some day marry a fine young man and give us some grandchildren."

Getting married was a subject she didn't want to discuss. So she ignored his comment and tried to convince him that what she was doing would change the world.

"Listen to me, Father. Women should be able to choose their own profession and receive equal education. Elizabeth Stanton feels we should have the right to vote and slavery should be abolished. After talking to her, I believe what she is doing is admirable and I want to follow in her footsteps. Did you know that Abigail Adams, the wife of John Adams, was the first woman to stand up for women's rights?"

"If it didn't work for Abigail way back then, how do you know it will work now?"

"We mustn't give up. We have a chance."

"Do you truly believe that?" her mother asked with concern.

Laura nodded. "I do. I really do."

With a sigh, her mother said, "I suppose we should support you because it's for a good cause." She turned to her husband. "What do you think?"

He nodded. "I agree. But I don't see how she can make a difference."

That was a day Laura would not forget. She had won a very important battle. Her parents had finally accepted her decision. Laura had convinced her parents that women's rights were worth fighting for. She was grateful for that because she wanted their support.

Looking up at the puffy clouds floating by, she said with spunk, "One day women will have the right to vote. I know it."

Linda Weaver Clarke

Chapter 2

Laura rose to her feet and headed for the house. It was time to fix a meal. As she opened the door, Laura felt a sense of uneasiness, like something was wrong. As she stood in the doorway, Laura wondered why she had such a peculiar feeling. For some reason, she sensed the presence of someone in her home. Whether it was women's intuition or divine help from above, she heeded the warning.

Acting quickly, she grabbed the broom from the closet and began searching her home. She could feel the anxiety rising within her, as she checked each room. When she found no one, Laura wondered if it was her imagination.

A feeling to check her bedroom once again came to her. Heeding the warning, she started for the staircase. With each step she took, Laura tried to be cautious. Tightening her grip on the broom, she continued to the top of the stairs. When she put her foot on the top step, it squeaked with the pressure. Laura halted, waiting, watching, and aware of every little sound.

As she cautiously stepped toward her bedroom door, Laura could feel the beating of her heart telling her to be careful. Peering around the doorway into her bedroom, she saw no one. When she entered the room, she checked every corner. If no one was in her home, why had she sensed it? Something was wrong.

Tightening the grip on her broom, she stepped to her bed and lifted the ruffle. Looking underneath, her eyes widened when she found a man crouched down and hiding. When he saw her staring at him, the man grinned as if he didn't think she could do a thing about his presence since he was larger in build and stronger.

Whether he was in her home to rob her or had other evil intentions, she didn't know. The anger and resentment that welled up inside her made her act quickly. With all the strength she had, Laura began whacking him out from under the bed.

"Get out of my house," she yelled. "Get out! Get out! Get out! Do you hear me?"

As she smacked him with her broom, the man quickly crawled out from under the bed and placed his hands over his head to protect himself. With each blow, he winced. He was not prepared for a strong and determined woman with a weapon in her hands.

Realizing he was defeated, he gave up and ran from the room, but Laura wasn't about to let him go so easily. She ran after him, beating him with the broom over and over again. He quickly dashed out of the house and headed for the road but she was close behind. As she pummeled him, the man yelped with each blow to the head. Picking up speed, he ran down the street.

Coming to a stop, she watched the man flee and disappear from sight.

When Laura turned around, she saw Preacher Armstrong standing on his porch and watching her with widened eyes. He acted confused at the scene he had just witnessed.

Giving a shrug, Laura said firmly, "That's the last time a traveling peddler comes to my house."

Holding back a mischievous smile, she walked to her home. For some reason, she enjoyed teasing her neighbor. He was such a serious man.

Laura realized she had to report the intruder. He could not get away with it. What if he tried to enter someone else's home and rob them? After washing up and changing into something more presentable, she hitched up her horse and buggy then headed toward the sheriff's office.

Pulling the horse to a stop, Laura tied the reins to a hitching post and strode into the office. "I want to report an intruder."

When the lawman turned around, he raised his brow curiously. Deputy Davies had curly brown hair, an olive complexion, and a pleasant smile that instantly got her attention.

Stepping toward her, he said, "Deputy William Davies, at your service. Sheriff Adamson is out of the office but should be back soon. May I help you, Miss McBride?"

When he called her by name, she was surprised since they had not been introduced. Listening to his Welsh accent was intriguing. It was so melodic as he spoke.

William's eyes brightened as he said, "I enjoyed your lecture that you gave last week at Town Square. You had quite a crowd. It was a good speech."

Laura raised her brow. "Are you serious? I was speaking to the women of Willow Valley."

"I know. But the subject got my interest so I stayed and listened."

"You're interested in the topic of women's rights?" she asked with disbelief.

"Yes, I am. My sister graduated from a private school in Wales. And now she teaches an evening class for adults, helping them to read and write. I'm proud of her accomplishments and what she's doing for the community. I believe women are every bit as capable as men."

"You do?" she asked with astonishment.

"You bet. My father taught us from a very young age to respect women. I don't believe all this rubbish that women don't need to vote. They need to have a say about things, too."

Laura was taken off guard by what he had just said and wasn't sure how to respond. She usually had to defend her beliefs. Most men challenged her. When they asked her what she knew about politics, she gave her opinion and they usually scoffed at her views. It was like throwing her pearls before swine. That was how the Bible described it.

She gazed at Deputy Davies with a tilt of her head. He intrigued her. "You are a very curious fellow, Deputy. Most men don't think it's proper for women to make speeches and give their opinions publicly. A Congregationalist Minister from Massachusetts wrote an article that said it was unwomanly and unchristian for a woman to speak publicly. He even said that it threatens our character."

"Balderdash!" exclaimed William as he furrowed his brow. "I don't believe it. It shows that a woman has character and courage to stand up for what she believes."

Laura smiled, enjoying his comments but wasn't sure how to respond. This was the first time she didn't have to defend herself.

"In your speech," he continued. "You mentioned that you received your education from Troy Seminary. The sheriff's wife taught at that school."

"Really? Is that so?"

"Absolutely."

Just at that moment, Felicity swung the door open and walked in with a basket in her hand. "I hope I'm not disturbing you, William. I brought something for you and Nicholas to snack on."

"What a coincidence! We were just talking about you." With a wide grin, he turned to Laura. "This is Felicity Adamson, the sheriff's wife." Turning to Felicity, he said, "This is Laura

McBride. I was telling her how you taught school at Troy Seminary."

"Yes, I did," said Felicity as she placed a small basket on the desk. "I taught in the arts program. When my father passed away, I came back home to help Mama adjust. I intended to go back but never did. My mother needed me."

"As it should be," said Laura with sympathy. "I'm sorry for your loss."

"Thank you. I heard that you gave a delightful speech last week. William told me all about it. I'm so sorry that I missed it."

Upon that news, she glanced at William and smiled. "I'm hoping to spread the word concerning women's rights. I don't think there are many of us. Hopefully the numbers will grow, though."

"No! You're wrong," exclaimed William with a shake of his head. "There are far more than you realize."

With surprise, Laura asked, "What do you mean?"

"You're not alone when it comes to women's rights here in Illinois. Just north of us, there's a group of people who believe in equality."

"There is?" asked Laura with stunned surprise.

"They teach the importance of education for women and encourage them to develop their talents. They even encourage them to get involved in politics and to give their opinion."

Laura was shocked. She had butted heads with many men. And the women were afraid to make waves in their marriage so they remained silent. She felt so alone with her opinions and in her crusade.

With great curiosity, Laura said, "Who are they, Deputy? I'd like to know more."

"William... please call me William. And yes, it's true. The women actually formed an organization called *The Female Relief Society* and they have hundreds of women who have joined them. Literally hundreds!"

Folding her arms, she asked with great interest, "What is their purpose?"

"They give relief to those who are poor by making clothes for their children. They seek out the distressed and sick and help them. They are a compassionate lot."

"Are they Quakers?" Laura shook her head. "No, they couldn't be. I actually had a Quaker chase me off his land and wouldn't allow me to teach independence to their women."

William laughed. "No, they aren't Quakers."

"Tell me about these women."

"They belong to a new religion just recently organized in the city of Nauvoo. The president of the society is Emma Hale Smith."

As she listened to William, Laura seemed drawn to him. It was probably because of his support in her cause. She had received so much opposition that it was refreshing to meet someone who supported her. He had actually listened to her lecture at Town Square. That was impressive.

Remembering her purpose for being in the sheriff's office, she went back to the subject at hand. "The reason I'm here is because someone invaded my home. I believe he heard me coming so he hid under my bed. When I found him, I swatted him out of the house with a broom and he got away."

"That's not what I heard," said Nicholas as he stood at the open doorway. "This young woman has spirit. Preacher Armstrong said you swatted that man all the way down the street. He said you gave him a real beating as you chased him, and he was yelping as he went."

"You chased him down the street?" exclaimed William with stunned surprise. "Really? You beat him with a broom?"

"I was mad. He snuck into my home." She shrugged her shoulders. "I couldn't let him get away that easily, so I pummeled him good."

A humorous smile tugged at William's lips. "I would have loved to have seen that."

"I sure wish you had been there," said Laura with spunk. "Then you could have caught him and put him behind bars."

Nicholas cocked his head curiously as he said, "So the man wasn't a peddler as the preacher thought?"

Laura tried to hold back a smile as she shook her head. "No. Preacher Armstrong is such a nosy fellow and he is always gossiping, so I decided to give him something fun to gossip about. I couldn't help it."

Nicholas broke into laughter. "William, will you please take this young lady's report? And get a good description of the man." Motioning to the basket, he said to his wife, "That smells good, sweetheart. It smells like fresh bread."

"It is," said Felicity as she walked into his arms and gave him a kiss.

Taking a pencil and paper, William headed for the door as he said, "Follow me, please."

He led Laura outside to the porch and they both took a seat on a bench.

Looking at the form in his hand, he cleared his throat and asked, "What's your given name, Miss McBride?"

She smiled, amused by his business-like tone. "Laura... Laura McBride."

After he wrote her name down, he looked up and asked, "Are you related to the former sheriff?"

"Yes. He's my uncle. He's the one who encouraged us to move here."

"He was a great sheriff. I liked him." Clearing his throat, William continued. "Age?"

"Twenty." Quickly, she added, "But I'll soon be twenty one."

He raised his brow as he wrote the information down. "Address?"

"401 Lilac Lane."

"Lilac Lane?" asked William with surprise. "That's just a few blocks from Sheriff Adamson's home. How long have you lived in Willow Valley?"

"Just over a month. My uncle found a house for us so we didn't hesitate and made the move."

As he put his pencil to the form, William said, "Description of the intruder, please."

Laura thought for a moment and then replied, "He has long brown hair, which was unkempt and shaggy, a brown beard, gray eyes, and he's short."

Looking up, he asked, "Shorter than you or shorter than the average man?"

Laura thought for a moment and said, "He's shorter than the average man. About my height."

"How about any distinguishing marks or anything unusual about him?"

As Laura thought about it, she nodded. "Yes. He has long wispy eyebrows swept upward and crooked yellow teeth. I assume he's a drinker because he has bags under his eyes, which is very noticeable."

William acted alarmed as he wrote down the description. "Is there anything else you can remember?"

"No, that's it." She studied his handsome face and asked, "Is something wrong?"

William shook his head, but she could tell that something was bothering him. After writing down the last bit of information, he placed his pencil and paper on the bench.

"You are so brave," he said with admiration. "I can't imagine how you must have felt when you discovered him in your home. I'm sure you were distressed and rather upset by his intrusion."

"Yes, I was. Father has some valuables that he's collected throughout the years. Thank goodness they're still packed. We haven't had time to unpack everything yet."

"Are you all right?" William asked with concern.

"I'm fine." Rising to her feet, she said, "Thank you, Deputy."

"It's William. Remember?"

"Yes, William."

He stood and followed Laura to her buggy. "Since we live next to the Mississippi with all the riverboats coming and going, we have a few vagabonds. The man you saw may be one of those. I hope you don't think Willow Valley is full of miscreants. It's actually a very friendly place."

When she noticed a look of concern in his eyes, Laura shook her head. "Oh, I like Willow Valley very much. It's a pretty little community."

"There's a lot to do here," said William as he spread his arms out, encompassing the area. "In case you didn't know, we have a town social every Saturday night with dancing and we have regular recitals at the cathedral. We also have a beautiful lake not far from here where all kinds of birds and ducks make their home. You'll have to check it out."

When he gave her a charming smile, Laura decided right then and there that she liked him. He didn't want her to feel unwelcome or threatened in Willow Valley.

"Thank you, William, for your concern. The intruder hasn't changed my feelings about Willow Valley one bit. I assure you."

"Good. I'm glad." Cocking his head curiously, he asked, "Do you enjoy dancing?"

Laura nodded. "Most definitely."

"The town social is this Saturday. I hope to see you there."

Giving a coy smile, she climbed into her buggy. "Perhaps. We'll see."

"Save me a dance?"

Taking the reins in her hand, she said in a teasing tone, "Perhaps!"

Chapter 3

Nicholas slammed his fist on the desk with frustration. When Sam jumped, William smiled at the young man. Sam was only twenty years of age and was going to attend college in Willow Valley, so he would be working only part time starting next week.

"I'm guessing that you're frustrated. Right?" William said with a smile tugging at the corners of his lips. "Let me guess. It has something to do with the thefts around town."

Nicholas furrowed his brow. "It sure does. Every time we get this many people in one place for a revival meeting, there's always trouble. I wish those people had picked somewhere else to have their blasted revivals. Not that I'm against a little religion, as you well know."

William couldn't help but smile because he understood. The sheriff went to church regularly but these revivals were different.

Pointing to the "wanted poster" on the desk and the form that William had filled out about Laura's intrusion, he said, "That's the same man, isn't it? It's the same description. His name is Frank McLaughlin, and he's wanted for horse theft and other sundry burglaries. I'm sure he's responsible for those stolen horses during the revival meeting yesterday."

"Maybe Frank is part of a gang, like those river pirates you caught a few years back," said Sam as his eyes brightened with interest.

"River pirates?" repeated Nicholas with a raised brow.

Sam nodded. "That's right. If it's a gang of pirates, they can easily steal what they want, put everything on a flatboat, and head down the river. What do you think?"

Nicholas shrugged his shoulders. "Don't know for sure. You may be right."

He sat down at his desk and started writing a note. Then he put it in an envelope and handed it to Sam.

"Take this note to Sheriff Carter down at Memphis. I've got some questions to ask him. I read that he had some horse thieves the same time they had a revival meeting at one of the plantations down there. Maybe Sheriff Carter will have more information." He handed Sam some cash and said, "You can take the riverboat. This should take care of your expenses."

Without hesitation, Sam headed out the door. He would probably be gone for a few days since it was a ways to travel.

William stepped to the window and watched the young man climb on his horse and leave. When Laura popped into his head without any warning, a smile played at the corners of his lips. He remembered her mischievous smile when she said she just *might* save him a dance.

The young lady intrigued him to no end. When he heard her teaching at Town Square, William was impressed. He had never met a woman so independent and confident. As he was passing by her home and heard her preaching to her daisies, he was quite amused.

He chuckled to himself as he remembered her response.

"What's on your mind?" asked Nicholas as he placed some papers in his desk drawer. "Do you have any suggestions?"

William blinked and turned around. "Did you say something, sir? Sorry. My mind was on something else. What would you like me to do?"

Nicholas grinned. "Do you happen to have a certain young lady on your mind?"

Cocking his head, William said innocently, "I'm not sure what you mean."

Nicholas laughed. "You have been quite distracted ever since Laura left. Just now you were gazing out the window and chuckled to yourself. I tend to draw a conclusion that Miss McBride may be the reason."

William laughed and quickly changed the subject. "Do you have any plans to catch the intruder?"

"Yes, I do. Could you please check out the revival meeting?" Pointing to the wanted poster, he said, "Search for Frank McLaughlin. If he's responsible for the thievery, he might be milling around and looking for more action. Tonight is the last night of the revival. Tomorrow is Sunday and everyone will be going home around noon. Thank goodness! This has been a weekend of frustration."

William knew that Nicholas did not like the camp meetings that were held at Willow Valley. They usually lasted for three days, from Friday to Sunday. Families would pitch their tents near a forest clearing and attend the meetings, which were usually held in the middle of a field.

Some people came out of curiosity but most yearned for religion. It was advertised so well that people from all over the valley attended, some traveling as far as thirty to forty miles to listen to the enthusiastic preaching. Some of the preachers called it the Great Awakening.

William had heard that over a thousand people had arrived in Willow Valley to attend the meetings. Counting Willow Valley citizens, the attendance was probably five to six thousand people who had gathered together to listen to the preachers. But that was small compared to some revivals. Many times 10,000 to 20,000 people attended because the preachers were so entertaining.

At the camp meetings, the itinerant preacher would read from the Bible, call everyone to repentance, give emotional sermons, sing hymns, and perform marriages and baptisms.

The overzealous preaching disturbed William. Being called to repentance and telling him how sinful he was didn't set well with him. When Nicholas gave him this assignment, he felt as if he was being punished. He wasn't looking forward to it.

"Don't look so glum, William," said Nicholas with a chuckle.

"Yeah, I know. It's part of being a deputy," responded William as he shook his head. "I don't think you could survive past the first ten minutes of their preaching. You would go crazy. As I think about it… better me than you."

Nicholas grinned. "I believe you're right."

"It's not that I don't appreciate a good sermon, Nicholas. I do. I go to church every Sunday and enjoy partaking of the sweet spirit there. But it's different at these revival meetings. I can't handle the emotions that come from those who are repenting. They groan and moan." He shook his head. "Enough said. I'll let you know what I find out."

As William walked through the doorway, he heard Nicholas laughing. He sure was amused.

Climbing upon his horse, he headed for the outskirts of town where the camp meeting was being held in a large open field. When he arrived, William noticed it was packed full of people. There was a platform constructed at each end of the field and a preacher was standing atop, giving an impassioned sermon to those who had congregated around him. The platforms were about eight to ten feet above the ground.

William recognized Preacher Armstrong who was giving a discourse to his congregation, but he didn't recognize the other preacher. Apparently he had come from out of town.

"And that's not all," said Preacher Armstrong in a strong and determined voice. "Many people think there isn't any harm in dancing and I agree, but there is one style of dancing that has snuck among us like a wolf in sheep's clothing. It has been introduced to us as the Boston Waltz. I want you to know that I denounce this new way of dancing. It can excite passions in our young people and give them undue familiarity with one another. Should a man take a young lady in his arms and twirl her around the room? No! We must stop this kind of wanton behavior. You and I must fight against it. Guard your children!"

William was shocked. Did he hear the preacher correctly? Did Armstrong denounce the waltz and say the waltz was sinful? He couldn't believe what he heard. Giving a shake of his head, he looked the congregation over and then meandered toward the other end of the field to listen to the second preacher. Hopefully his message would be more positive and not so scathing.

As he scanned the congregation to see if he could find Frank McLaughlin, a man nudged him and pointed to the preacher. "Isn't he wonderful? He's one of the best preachers we've heard around these parts. No one wants him to leave."

Glancing up at the preacher, William could tell he was an Irishman because of his accent. "Who is he?"

"Preacher McGrath. He's a Methodist preacher from Mississippi, and he travels around the country giving sermons. Last night, he baptized my children and promised them prosperity and wealth."

Raising his brow, William said with doubt, "How can he promise them wealth?"

The man shrugged. "The holy spirit told him so."

William gave a deep sigh. The people had a great deal of faith in this preacher. "I don't think God cares about wealth," said William. "But that's just my opinion."

As he walked around the field, looking for Frank, he listened to the preacher. The man was full of life. Standing on his platform, he sang a hymn then the congregation enthusiastically joined in. After that, he preached an emotional sermon, similar to Preacher Armstrong's speech. A few people shouted "amen" at something he said, causing others to shout, as well.

William winced when he heard Preacher McGrath give a long loud groan, as if he were overcome with the Holy Spirit. Then he told the congregation to repent of their sins. Apparently, he wasn't any different than Armstrong.

Afterwards, McGrath climbed down from his platform and strolled among the people as if searching for someone. When he came to a halt, he touched an individual on the head, saying a short prayer, as if he were able to save his soul.

Glancing over at Armstrong, William noticed that the preacher was leading his congregation in a lively hymn, which attracted several people who wandered in his direction.

As he watched the people and their reactions to the preachers, it looked as if they admired these men. Most ministers weren't usually so animated.

At that moment, he saw the man whom Laura had described, so he headed in Frank's direction. When the bearded man saw him coming, he quickly slipped into the crowd. A few men stood up just as he passed by them, hiding him from view.

Taking long strides, William hurried in the direction where Frank had gone, but the man had disappeared through the trees.

As he searched among the woods, he wondered if Frank had noticed that he was a deputy. Was that why he fled? Was he part of a pirate gang as Sam had suspected? Walking out from the trees, he looked at the men who had blocked his way. Was it just a coincidence that they stood up just as Frank passed by?

The first night of the revival, twenty horses had been stolen. What would happen tonight?

When William heard groaning come from the platform, he turned around and saw Preacher McGrath pointing at him. "Woe... woe be unto the sinner if you do not change your wanton ways. Repent ye, repent ye!"

William's eyes widened at the rebuke. The preacher was looking directly at him. Without hesitation, McGrath burst into song. Soon everyone joined in and sang along with him. The enthusiastic singing filled the air.

As he watched the preacher, William remembered what his friend, Lucas Golden, had told him. *Beware! Revivalists tend to get quite dramatic.* And he was definitely right.

After Preacher McGrath's sermon was over, he turned to his helpers and said, "Pass around a bowl so my congregation can drop some money in as a donation."

When one of the men approached him with the bowl, William shook his head and motioned for him to continue on his way.

The man furrowed his brow and frowned. "Suit yourself. If you don't want any blessings, it's up to you."

William didn't respond. He was so frustrated that he had let Frank slip away.

Raising his voice, the preacher said to his audience, "I have heard your pleas for my return, and I thank you for your generous donations. As to your request, I promise to return in two weeks for another camp meeting. Bring your loved ones and family members. And don't forget your pocket books so you can help fund this trip once again."

William knew Nicholas would not be happy with that announcement. He hated it when the town was swarming with people because that was when the most crime happened. The only thing he had to report was that Frank McLaughlin was among the people but had disappeared into the woods.

William knew he was milling around the camp to rob those with plenty. It certainly was not to get a little religion.

Then it dawned on him. There was one more day of revival meetings. William was sure that Nicholas was going to assign him to be on duty Sunday morning until the preachers left at noon. At that moment, William realized he needed to be strong to endure it.

As he thought about it, he did have a well-trained voice. Maybe if he sang the hymns along with the congregation, time would pass more quickly.

Chapter 4

It was Monday evening and Laura was preparing for her lecture at the cathedral. She was supposed to speak to the youth of the community. She wanted the young women to know what lay ahead in their future. To say she was nervous was an understatement. She had spoken to many women about the subject, but this would be her first time to speak to the youth.

Pulling up to the cathedral, she noticed that the crowd was already arriving and she was a half hour early. She sat in her buggy, trying to calm her racing heart. Why was she so nervous? Was it because these were young teenagers and she wanted to make a difference in their lives? She needed to calm down.

"Good evening, Miss McBride," said a deep familiar voice.

When she turned around, William was standing beside her buggy. She couldn't help but notice his charming smile.

"You look lovely this evening," said William as he held out his hand, offering to help her down.

Laura took his hand with a raise of her brow, wondering if he was still on duty.

As he helped her down from the buggy, William said, "We're having lovely weather, aren't we? Not too cold, not too warm."

Amused at his subject, Laura laughed. "Oh yes. It's very nice, indeed. Were you just passing by?"

He shook his head. "Not passing by. My sister wanted to attend your lecture so I volunteered to drive her to the cathedral. She's already inside." With a shrug of his shoulders, he said, "Since I'm here, I might as well stay and listen."

That surprised and pleased her at the same time. Why it made a difference that he was staying, she was not sure. Laura liked him but... she was promised to another.

Holding out his arm toward her, he said, "Shall I walk you inside?"

With a smile, she took his arm and they headed across the street toward the cathedral.

Glancing at her, William said, "Wonderful weather we're having, isn't it?"

She laughed. "Yes, it is. I believe we already covered that subject."

"Oh yes." He smiled as if embarrassed. "I did mention that, didn't I?"

When William chuckled, she noticed that his laughter was warm and full of life. She liked it.

As they entered the building, he gave her a wink and said, "I'll be sitting in the balcony with my sister. Good luck."

Laura shook her head. "I don't need luck."

With that said, she walked to the front of the cathedral where Angelica was waiting for her.

Giving her a hug, Angelica said, "I'm so excited. Our young women need to know what kind of future they can look forward to. I want them to know they have rights." She motioned to her husband sitting in the front row. "Simon wants to interview you afterwards."

Laura had heard that Angelica's husband owned the Willow Valley News and she was pleased that he was interested in interviewing her.

Angelica led her to the stage and they both sat down, waiting for the meeting to begin. As the minutes ticked by, Laura took the time to look at the youth. They seemed excited to be here. That was a good sign. Looking down at her notes, Laura ran over her speech in her mind, hoping to not forget everything she wanted to say.

After a while, Angelica stood and introduced their guest speaker.

"Welcome, ladies!" When Angelica looked up at the balcony and saw William, she smiled and quickly added, "And gentlemen. You are going to have a treat tonight. I can promise you that. Laura McBride graduated from Troy Seminary in New York. After graduating, she decided to follow the path of Elizabeth Stanton. Laura has been teaching about the subject of equality for two years now. With no further ado, I give you Laura McBride."

The young girls were excited as they whispered back and forth and nodded their heads.

When Laura stood and walked to the pulpit, everyone settled down and all was silent. Taking a deep breath, she began.

"Our ancestors came to America seeking freedom and equality. We didn't want to be ruled by a king. We wanted to vote for our own laws. Am I right?" Laura shook her head. "Not quite. How about the women? They were part of the Revolutionary War, too. Many helped in ways that would surprise you. So why don't we have the same privileges? Why can't we have a say in politics? Why can't we vote?"

After getting the attention of the young women, Laura continued her talk, encouraging the youth to develop their talents and to make a difference in the world.

Her speech went well and the young women clapped enthusiastically. When the room was finally empty, Simon interviewed her. It was refreshing to talk to someone from the newspaper who was so supportive. It wasn't usually the case. They always criticized her for speaking out, saying it was not womanly to give lectures.

Laura was exhausted when the interview was over. After bidding Angelica and Simon farewell, she wearily headed down the steps of the cathedral. She noticed the lampposts were lit as she walked to her buggy. To her surprise, there stood Deputy Davies.

Tilting her head curiously, she said, "Weren't you supposed to drive your sister home?"

"I already did. We don't live far from here." He gave a slight shrug and smiled. "I wanted to tell you how much I enjoyed your lecture. My sister said it was the best speech she has ever heard and it gave her hope for a better future. She especially liked what you said about developing your talents." Glancing at his horse, he gave a shrug. "Well, I'd best be on my way. You look tired and I'm keeping you up."

She was touched that he had come all the way back just to tell her how much he and his sister enjoyed her speech.

As he turned to leave, she touched his arm and said, "I'm not that tired. Stay a while. Let's visit. Or do you have a pressing engagement?"

He understood her invitation and chuckled. Leaning against Laura's buggy, he gazed up at the sky and said, "We're having lovely weather, aren't we? Not too cold, not too warm."

The weather seemed to be a popular subject for some reason. Was he nervous around her? The thought amused her. Why would he be nervous? He was so darned good-looking that she figured he had several women vying for his attention.

Glancing at her, William said, "The stars are shining brighter than usual. I don't see a cloud in the sky."

Looking up at the stars, she nodded. "You're right. They are bright."

"When I was young, I enjoyed learning about the constellations," said William as he motioned to the stars. "One year for my birthday, Mother gave me a book that taught me each group and their names."

Laura sighed as a memory came rushing back to her. "On the day of my tenth birthday, my father took me outside and told me that the heavens were celebrating my birthday. I never forgot that day. Shooting stars were falling from the heavens like they had never done before."

William turned to her and said, "I've seen a few shooting stars but not many. Mother told me if I made a wish before it disappeared, it would come true."

"Oh my! You could have made thousands of wishes with what I saw that night."

William cocked his head curiously. "Thousands? What do you mean?"

"It was a sight to behold, William. On the day of my birthday, November twelfth, 1833, the stars were falling from the heavens so fast that it looked like it was raining stars. Some people described it as burning snowflakes falling from the heavens. It was so beautiful. It was estimated between 100,000 and 200,000 meteors fell each hour."

William's eyes widened. "Each hour? Are you serious?"

She nodded.

"That's a lot. I remember reading about it, and I always wondered if it was an exaggeration because it was only seen in America."

"Oh, it wasn't an exaggeration. It actually happened," said Laura as she spread her arms out to encompass the sky. Turning to William, she laughed. "I will never forget that day. My father told me that some people were in awe, just like we were. But it terrified others. Some thought it was the end of the world. They actually thought it was Judgment Day. Can you believe that?"

"Well, it does say in the Bible that the stars would fall from the heavens when it's time for the Lord's Second Coming. I can see why they were frightened." He grinned and his eyes were full of mirth. "They were probably putting off their repentance, just like Preacher McGrath was preaching at his revival meeting. He actually pointed at me, telling me to repent."

"You went to the revival?" she asked with surprise.

He groaned. "I was on duty, looking for the man who broke into your home. For two days, I had to listen to a call for repentance, with moaning and groaning from those who regretted their decisions in life."

Laura bit her lip and shook her head with amusement. "It sounds like you didn't enjoy it."

William shook his head vigorously. "No, I didn't. So tell me about these falling stars that you witnessed. I'd like to know more. All these years I wondered if the article I read was really true. I can only imagine what it was like to see so many stars falling from the heavens."

"For me, I was filled with wonderment, but it affected everyone differently. Father said that some people wept and feared for their lives. Many knelt in prayer, repenting of their sins. It was reported that some plantation owners were so frightened that they called their servants and slaves together and apologized for the way they had been treated, asking their forgiveness. Then they told them where they could find their parents. It really put the fear of God in them."

William sighed. "It is such a shame that it took something like that to make people realize how wrong they had been. That night changed a lot of people, didn't it?"

She nodded. "Most everyone refers to it as *The Night the Stars Fell*. But I remember it as the night we celebrated my tenth birthday."

William chuckled. As he looked up at the sky, he said, "I sure wish I could have seen it."

"If you had, you could have made thousands of wishes."

He shook his head. "It never worked when I was a boy. So I gave up on making wishes."

Laura laughed. "Just because it didn't come true instantly doesn't mean that it won't come true eventually."

William gazed into her eyes and smiled. "Did you make a thousand wishes that night?"

Laura shook her head. "It was such a magnificent sight that the idea of making a wish didn't even enter my mind. I never thought about it until it was over." She looked up at the sky and grinned. "Can you imagine how many wishes I could have made?"

William broke into laughter.

After a moment, Laura said, "Well, I guess I should go. It's getting late. I enjoyed our little visit. Let's do it again."

William took her hand and helped her climb into the buggy. Giving her fingers a gentle squeeze, he said, "Don't forget to save me a dance on Saturday."

Ignoring the fluttering of her heart, she said with a coy smile, "Perhaps."

With that said, she jiggled the reins and the horse took off down the street. All the way home, she couldn't get William off her mind. He wasn't like other men, thinking women were too fragile to do anything but housework or too feeble-minded to vote for a politician. He even supported his sister when she wanted to teach an evening class for adults.

Laura was definitely interested in getting to know him better.

Linda Weaver Clarke

Chapter 5

The following day Laura gathered all the fliers she had printed and placed them in her bag, along with some tacks and a hammer. She needed to distribute them so the word would get out by Friday. After hitching up her buggy, she placed the bag on the seat and climbed in. Giving a snap to the reins, she headed to her friend's home, hoping she could help. Mary had volunteered her services and hopefully she wouldn't be too busy.

As Laura pulled her buggy up to her friend's home, she noticed that she was sitting on the porch. She was a dear friend and Laura was grateful for her friendship. Mary was a beautiful woman. Her dark brown hair was thick and her brown eyes had warmth that made people feel comfortable around her. Sadly, she was a widow. Her husband had died of pneumonia and left her with an adorable eight-year-old son.

When Mary saw Laura, her eyes brightened as she got to her feet and stepped down from the porch. "What a wonderful surprise," said Mary as she approached the buggy.

Laura climbed down and smiled warmly. "I could really use your help."

"Of course. What can I do for you this fine day?"

She handed Mary a bunch of flyers. "Would you please spread these around town? I'm having a meeting on Friday at Town Square."

"Of course!" replied Mary as she looked at the flyers. "Oh my! If this doesn't grab the hearts of the women, nothing will. They would have to have cold hearts to not be affected by this message."

On each flyer was a picture of a coin. On the coin was a woman kneeling and looking heavenward with her chained hands clasped together, as if praying.

The words on the coin read: *Am I not a woman and a sister?* Below the picture, Laura had written: *No matter our race or color, all men are created equal in the sight of God.*

"Good subject," said Mary. "You do know it's dangerous being an abolitionist this close to the southern states, don't you?"

Laura nodded. She knew what she was getting herself into. And she was grateful Illinois had many others just like her.

She pointed to the coin and said, "This grabbed at my heart, so I decided to include it in the flyer."

"I like it," said Mary. "When you spoke on women's rights last night, you had a great turnout. What kind of attendance are you expecting for this lecture?"

Laura shrugged. "I don't know. I've got Angelica helping me. She and her husband are hanging flyers in some nearby towns so I thought you and I could cover Willow Valley."

Mary grinned and the enthusiasm could be seen in her face. "Sounds good to me."

"Thank you," said Laura with heartfelt gratitude. "I'll cover all the stores at Town Square, and you can take Main Street and those shops. Is that all right with you?"

Mary nodded. "You might have a bigger turnout than expected."

"I hope so. I've only got a few days to prepare. Friday will be here all too soon."

Teasingly, Mary said, "William told me that he heard you rehearsing your speech to the daisies."

Laura groaned. "I didn't expect anyone to pass by."

"He thought you were adorable."

Laura laughed. Giving Mary a quick hug, she said, "Talk to you later."

Climbing into her buggy, she headed toward Town Square. After finding a good place to park, she took her hammer, tacks, and a handful of flyers and began hanging them up at all the shops. Then she hung a few in the park and at the gazebo.

When she was done, Laura sat on a park bench and contemplated where she should go next. When a couple of women stopped and read the flyer tacked to the gazebo, Laura overheard their remarks and it made her smile.

"I heard her speak at the cathedral," said an elderly woman. "I took my granddaughter so she could hear what this lovely woman had to say about our rights. Miss McBride knows what she's talking about. She's a pretty little thing. Mark my words! It's this next generation that's going to make a difference in the world."

As the women left, Laura saw Deputy Davies ride up. He was such a good-looking man and well built, too. She smiled when he waved to her.

After climbing down from his horse, he tied it to a hitching post and walked toward her. "Fancy seeing you here," said William cheerfully. "How are you doing?"

"I'm fine, thank you." Holding up the flyers, she said, "I'm trying to promote my upcoming lecture."

Taking one of the flyers from her hand, he read it. Raising a brow, he said, "Good subject. Would you like some help?"

"Thank you for the offer but aren't you on duty?"

"Yes, I am. But it's my duty to help the citizens of Willow Valley. I know some places that would be perfect for these. Stores aren't the only place to put up flyers. How about it? Could you use some help?"

Laura's eyes brightened as she got to her feet. "All right. I accept your offer."

William held out his arm and she took it.

After helping her into the buggy, he said, "I'll take you to some places that you probably never thought of."

Climbing in, he took the reins and headed south. When he pulled up to Doctor Lucas Golden's office, she turned to William and tilted her head curiously. Was he serious? She had only thought of placing flyers at stores.

Helping her down, he looked at the flyer in her hand and shook his head. "No. We're not going to hang it up. We're going to put a pile on his desk where all his patients can take one home to show their friends. It will remind them of the lecture. You don't want them to forget about it, do you?"

A smile split across her face as she nodded. "Good idea! Why didn't I think of that?"

Grinning, he replied, "That's why you have me along."

With that said, she pulled out a stack of flyers from her bag and headed up the porch. As they walked inside, she saw plenty of patients waiting for the good doctor.

When William motioned for her to place them on the desk, she asked, "Shouldn't we ask permission first?"

He shook his head. "Lucas is busy and I hate to bother him. I'm sure it'll be fine. I've seen many a flyer laying on his desk."

"Just the same, I'd like to know if he approves."

As Lucas walked out of his office with a patient, he said with a Kentucky accent, "You should be better by the end of the week, if you do as I suggested."

"Thank you, Doc," said the gentleman. "I appreciate it."

Lucas turned to William and smiled. "Good day, my friend. What can I do for you?"

Handing him a flyer, William said, "We'd like to place a bunch of these on your desk for your patients."

He read it and nodded. "Most certainly. This is for a good cause. I've heard this young lady is stirring things up in our city." He chuckled. "And it's about time! We're in a rut and someone needs to get us out of it." Turning to Laura, he asked, "Are you, by any chance, the young lady who is giving this lecture?"

She nodded. "Yes, sir. I am. I'm Laura McBride."

"I'm glad to finally meet you. My wife told me all about your lecture at the cathedral. She took our sixteen-year-old niece, Josie, and they were so impressed. My wife loved how you encouraged the youth to develop their talents."

Laura blushed at the praise and said, "Why, thank you, sir. I was nervous because it was my first time to speak to the youth. And I hoped they understood my message."

"Oh yes. Josie plays the piano and went away with a determination to develop her talent." Glancing at his patients, he said, "Well, I've got to get back to work."

After placing a pile of flyers on his desk, William held the door open for Laura.

As they walked to the buggy, she said, "Coming here was just what I needed. Hearing how Josie enjoyed the lecture really lifted my spirits. I needed that little boost. Thank you."

William smiled as he helped her into the buggy. "I'm glad I could help."

After climbing in beside her, he took the reins and gave a snap. The next place he stopped was at the sheriff's office.

When she turned to him with a questioning look, he laughed. "I know what you're thinking. But it's a good place for flyers. Do you know how many people come here on a daily basis... reporting problems and needing help? Trust me. It's perfect."

He took some flyers from her bag and climbed down from the buggy just as the sheriff walked outside. "Good day, Nicholas! Miss McBride has some flyers that she wants to leave on your desk. And she would like to hang one on the door, too."

With a teasing glint in his eyes, Nicholas said, "I see you're helping one of our Willow Valley citizens."

William gave a shrug of his shoulders. "Since she's new in town, I thought I could help by showing her all the best places to hang her flyers."

Turning to Laura, Nicholas smiled. "Good day, Miss McBride. My wife went to your lecture at the cathedral last night and really enjoyed it. Felicity said she expected nothing less from a Troy Seminary graduate."

Laura laughed. "Why, thank you, Sheriff."

After handing the flyers to Nicholas, William took the hammer from Laura's bag and tacked one on the door. Turning to her, his chocolate brown eyes softened. The way he looked at her touched her heart and his charming smile seemed to pull her right into his world.

As he climbed into the buggy, he announced, "I have another place that is perfect."

"You do?"

Snapping the reins, the horse took off toward Town Square.

When he pulled up to Hannah's Hot Chocolate Shoppe, she said, "I already put a flyer next to the door. See?"

He shook his head as he climbed out of the buggy. "But you didn't place a bunch inside, did you? Do you know how many people stop by every day? They can take one home to show their friends. As I said before, it's a good reminder."

Laura laughed at his enthusiasm. This man was quickly finding a place in her heart with no effort at all. She bit her lip and told her beating heart to be still.

When William held out his hand to her, she took it. Lifting her skirts, she stepped down from the buggy.

Looking up into his dark eyes, she said, "Thank you, William. I appreciate your help."

"I'm glad to do it. After all, it's a deputy's duty to help the citizens of Willow Valley."

She laughed at his sense of humor.

After taking a bunch of flyers from her bag, she followed William inside the shop.

A waitress stood behind the counter and smiled as they approached. With an English accent, she said, "Welcome to Hannah's Hot Chocolate Shoppe! How may I help you?"

Pointing to the lady, William said, "I'd like to introduce you to Hannah. She owns this shop."

"She does?" Laura said with stunned surprise.

Was he serious? The woman standing in front of her actually owned this shop? That news was unexpected. She didn't know many women who owned their own business. Hannah was doing the very thing Laura was teaching... developing her talents.

Turning to William, Hannah said with laughter in her voice, "Nicholas told me that you've been checking out the revival meetings. How was it?"

William chuckled and shook his head. "If you like singing one hymn after another and being called to repentance, I'm sure you'd like it just fine."

Hannah broke into laugher.

Motioning to the flyers in Laura's hands, he said, "Could we leave a bunch of these on your counter?" Taking a flyer, he handed it to her. "Would your customers be interested in this?"

She read the flyer and her eyes brightened. "Of course. It looks like a worth-while event."

"Good." Taking the flyers from Laura, he placed them on the counter. "This is the young lady who will be lecturing at Town Square."

Hannah nodded. "It's nice to meet you. I would love to hear what you have to say on this subject. Maybe I can close shop early so I can attend."

Placing some coins on the counter, William said, "Two hot chocolates, please." Turning to Laura, his eyes brightened. "You're going to love this drink. It's like nothing you've ever tasted in your life. I promise."

Realizing she was intrigued with the idea of drinking hot chocolate, she accepted. "Thank you, William."

Placing more coins on the counter, he said, "I'd like a pie but not a slice... a whole pie. We'll share it, so give us two forks, please."

Hannah laughed. "You're one of my favorite customers. You love my pies almost as much as my hot chocolate."

With that said, she placed a pie on the counter with two forks. Then she scooped some hot chocolate into two mugs and placed them on the counter.

Taking the pie and forks to a small table, he said, "You're going to love it."

Laura grabbed hold of the hot chocolate mugs and sat down across from William.

Grinning from ear to ear, he took his mug and sipped his chocolate. Looking up at her, he hummed, "Mmm-hmm! Delicious!"

When Laura saw the expectant look in his eyes, she knew he was waiting for her. After taking a sip, Laura instantly realized why he loved it.

"Well? What do you think?"

"Delicious. I haven't tasted anything like it before."

"That's exactly what I thought." Handing her a fork, he said, "Dig in!"

As they sipped their chocolate and ate the apple pie, they talked and got to know one another. She noticed that William had a great sense of humor and she enjoyed his company. Each time he touched her hand, warmth enveloped her. That confused her because they were just friends.

"How about Main Street?" asked William. "Should we do that next?"

Laura shook her head. "No. Mary is doing that part of town for me."

"She's such a sweetheart," William said with warmth. "Mary has had a lot of trials in her life.

She amazes me. With all of her hardships, she still has such a positive attitude. I guess she told you everything she's been through."

Laura raised her brow curiously. "The only thing I know is that her husband died of pneumonia. Is there more?"

"Much more."

"Really?" Laura said with surprise. "When we get together, we mostly talk about my lectures and how prejudice can rule a person's life."

"That sounds like her. She has had to deal with prejudice a few times."

Tilting her head curiously, Laura asked, "What do you mean?"

William placed his fork on the empty pie tin and folded his arms over his broad chest. "Prejudice is a wicked thing. It eventually leads to harassment and abuse, both mentally and physically. Many times it can end up with violence. I believe prejudice drags down our society."

Giving a nod, Laura said, "I agree."

"A year after her husband's death, a mob invaded Mary's home and threatened her. When she didn't cower to their demands, they burned her home to the ground. She was homeless, Laura. So she moved to Willow Valley where her friends provided a place for her to live."

Laura sucked in her breath with stunned surprise. "I don't understand. Why would they do such a thing?"

"It was because of her religious beliefs. The men stormed into her home and demanded that she denounce her religion. Since you know what kind of woman she is, it won't surprise you to know that she stood up to them. With as much spunk as she could muster, she told them to burn it and be damned!"

Laura smiled at her friend's spunk. "That sounds like her."

"They gave her twenty minutes to get out of the house with what belongings she could carry with her. Then they burned it to the ground."

"But I don't understand. I'm confused. Why were they so upset with her religious views?"

William sipped his hot chocolate and placed the mug on the table. "For two reasons. First, this new Christian religion believes women have the same rights as men. They encourage them to get involved. That is one subject the world doesn't and won't agree upon. Women aren't equal to men."

"Oh, that makes me so frustrated," said Laura as she furrowed her brow. "I've received so much criticism because of my beliefs. I've even had a minister call me down for it, telling me that it's unchristian to make speeches in public. I should get married and leave the speeches to the men."

William laughed. "Sorry. I don't mean to make light of your situation. But what man would defend women's rights? If not you, then who?"

Laura smiled at his statement. For that very reason, she was drawn to him. Just looking into his chocolate brown eyes made her heart flutter.

Licking her lips, she cleared her throat and said, "So far I haven't had anyone try to hurt me because of my beliefs. Verbally, they've been cruel. But I haven't been harmed."

He placed his hand on hers and gave it a gentle squeeze. Warmth instantly enveloped her. She was surprised that his touch was affecting her senses. She hardly knew the man.

After a moment, William said, "Now for the second reason. Mary's new religion teaches something that greatly upsets the Missourians. The leader of her church teaches that slavery is wrong. It is a sin. Joseph Smith said that all men and women are equal in the eyes of God."

"He actually said that?" Laura said with disbelief.

"You bet. Joseph is sort of an abolitionist and he spoke out against slavery every chance he got. He was the epitome of a true Christian and believed that everyone is a child of God. When those of a different culture or race went to him, he lovingly took them into his home so he could help them. Unfortunately, he was martyred for his beliefs."

Laura's eyes widened with surprise. "I've met some ministers who say we mustn't rock the boat. They're afraid to take sides." Laura wrapped her hands around her mug of hot chocolate and shook her head with disgust. "I don't agree with the laws and I want to change them by giving lectures. If enough people fight against it, the laws can be changed. Don't you think?"

William leaned toward her and nodded. "I agree. You have the spunk to get the job done."

She laughed. "Father told me to be patient. He believes the laws will eventually be changed. But I don't think they will change if we don't take a stand and let it be known how we feel. Am I right?"

He squeezed her hand and smiled. "Absolutely."

The way he was gazing into her eyes, his charming smile, and the touch of his hand undid her. Pulling her hand free, she cleared her throat and said, "I have a question."

"And what's that?"

"This is the first time I've heard of a religion that isn't afraid to speak out for injustice. Are you saying they're being persecuted because of their beliefs?"

"That's exactly what I'm saying. When Mary and her husband joined the church, they moved to Missouri where others of her Faith were gathering. Just five years ago, Governor Boggs sent out a decree saying that all members of the church were to be run out of the state or be exterminated if they didn't leave. It didn't matter to him."

"Exterminated?" Laura gasped. "Oh my!"

"He sent the militia to make sure it was done. In the dead of winter... with snow covering the ground... over 5,000 people were forced to leave their homes. Some just had the clothes on their backs because the militia stole their belongings. It took one week to cross the plains into Illinois, and some didn't even have shoes so they had to wrap their feet with cloth."

Laura furrowed her brow. "How can a governor do that? This is America, the land of the free."

"But he did it and got away with it."

Laura wanted to weep for her friend. She didn't realize what Mary had gone through. It was so unfair. Looking up into his eyes, she said with spunk, "I would have fought back. Why didn't they?"

William sighed. "I often wondered that myself. They could have because there were more of them than the militia and they had the weapons. But they are a peace-loving people. So they agreed to give up and leave. After crossing the Mississippi, the kind citizens of Quincy took in the refugees and fed and cared for them until they were able to get back on their feet. The citizens of Quincy are a good and compassionate people."

"This is unbelievable," said Laura with soberness. "How did the governor get away with something like that?"

William shrugged his shoulders. "It's sad that we have so much violence, just because of a difference in opinion."

Tilting her head, she asked, "What's the name of this new religion? I'm curious."

William sipped the last of his hot chocolate and sat it on the table. "It's got a long name. Quite long, indeed. It's called The Church of Jesus Christ of Latter-day Saints."

As Laura thought about it, she was speechless. A group of people was being persecuted because of their beliefs. She, too, was preaching about a topic that was causing much discontent... equal rights for women. Not to mention her crusade against slavery and involuntary servitude.

Would her life be in danger, as well? Since Mary was kicked out of her home because of her beliefs, what would they do to her? She didn't want fear to rule her life. If it did, she wouldn't be as effective in her lectures.

Linda Weaver Clarke

Chapter 6

The following day, William walked into the sheriff's office around noon after completing an assignment. He was about to take a seat and rest when he saw the sober look on the sheriff's face.

Nicholas looked up from his paperwork and frowned. "I've got another assignment for you, Will. Someone came in and reported a disturbance over at Town Square. Could you please check it out for me?"

"You bet! What kind of disturbance is it?"

"Not sure. I was just told that a group of women are causing some trouble."

With a raise of his brow, he turned around and headed out the door. Curiosity drove him more than anything. Giving a kick to his horse, William took off down the road. As he passed the schoolhouse, William noticed Laura's buggy. She had mentioned that Miss Hart asked her to talk to her students. When she told him about it, Laura seemed quite elated and said that speaking to the children would be fun.

When he pulled up to Town Square, William immediately saw the problem. After tying his reins to a hitching post, he headed over to the group of women. There were about two-dozen of them. They were all seated on the boardwalk in front of the Butcher's Shop, barring the entrance so no one could enter. Some held signs that read: Equality!

As he walked up to the women, he asked, "Can someone tell me what's going on here?"

Before anyone could speak, the butcher yelled from the window, "They are preventing customers from coming inside. That's what they're doing. Get rid of them, Deputy!"

Turning to the women, William asked once again, "Who wants to tell me what's going on?"

All at once, several women tried to explain and outshout one another.

One woman chanted: "Equality! Equality! Equality!"

William laughed and held up his hand. "Whoa, ladies! This won't do." When it quieted down, he said, "All I need is one person to explain. Why are you sitting in the doorway? Any volunteers?"

"Let Miss Anthony explain," called out a young woman. "Susan organized this rebellion."

Susan got to her feet and said, "As you know, these are tough times for some of us. Some of the men are being laid-off for one reason or another and need to find a job." She pointed to a woman sitting beside her. "For my cousin, Sally, it's different. Her husband can't get a job because he was injured at work. It will be a long time before he can work again. So, leaving her children with her husband, she went out looking for a job."

The women all nodded as they watched their leader speak.

Pointing to a sign in the window that read: Help Wanted, she continued. "When Sally applied for a job here, the butcher said he couldn't use her. He needed a professional who could cut meat. When Sally explained that her father had trained her, he adamantly refused to hire her. She can do the job but he refuses to hire her because she's a woman."

"I don't hire women," yelled the butcher from his window. "I have the right to refuse anyone I want."

Turning to the butcher, Susan said, "And we have the right to tell everyone that you're prejudiced and to not buy from you."

"Get them out of here, Deputy! I have rights."

William understood what she was saying. The butcher was wrong. But he had a duty to keep the peace in Willow Valley. What was he to do?

Holding up his hand to quiet them down, he said, "To block a person's residence or place of business so no one can enter is against the law. But... if you stand to the side of the door and hold up your signs, there's no law against that. You can even encourage those who are about to enter to not buy from this man. But to take the free agency away from others by preventing them to enter the building is against the law. So what do you say, ladies? Do you agree to that arrangement?"

When Susan turned around and looked at the women, everyone nodded except for three women who sat directly in front of the door.

The one in the center shook her head and said firmly, "I don't agree. I'm here to make a statement. Allowing others to walk inside doesn't agree with me."

"I agree with Myrtle," said the woman beside her.

"I'm not budging either," said another.

"I'm staying right where I am," announced Myrtle. "You'll have to arrest me."

William sighed. "What statement are you making if you land in jail?"

Myrtle grinned. "My husband will know that I mean business. He didn't think I would fight for women's rights, but he's wrong. I'm not budging."

Susan turned to the women. "It's up to you. Do what you think is best. But make sure you tell every woman who comes up these steps what this butcher has refused to do. They have to know that women have rights." Then she lifted her chin high and said, "This is just the beginning. We must fight prejudice and inequality. One day women will vote. Even if I, Susan B. Anthony, have to get arrested for it… I will cast in my vote. You'll see!"

"Here! Here!" yelled Myrtle.

"*Resistance to tyranny is obedience to God*," called out Susan. "Remember that!"

Her cousin stood up and said, "That's an excellent statement. I'll remember it. If you had your own newspaper in New York, you could spread the word of all this injustice."

Susan cocked her head. "That's not a bad idea. When I go back to Rochester, I'll have to consider it."

"All right, ladies," said William. "It's up to you. What do you choose to do?"

Most of the women got to their feet and stood to the side of the doorway and some walked to the street with their signs in hand. The three stubborn women remained seated in front of the door with their arms folded in defiance.

William had never arrested a woman but it was his duty to uphold the law. If he acted unsure of himself, the women wouldn't listen to him. The last thing he wanted was to have the sheriff think he couldn't do his responsibility and was incompetent.

Taking a deep breath, he said with authority and as much courage as he could muster, "All right, ladies! Since you refuse to obey the law, you're under arrest. Please follow me." When they didn't budge, he stared down at Myrtle. "I have no other choice. It's my duty. Will you please lead the way?"

Myrtle stared up at him as she pressed her lips together in defiance.

William didn't take his eyes off her but waited. "Please? I believe in your cause but I have to uphold the law."

After a moment, Myrtle softened. Glancing at her friends, she gave a nod. All three women finally stood.

With a breath of relief, William said, "Please follow me, ladies."

When Susan saw he was about to leave, she walked up to him and said, "Thank you for your support, Deputy. I appreciated what you said."

He smiled. "Glad to be of assistance. I would like to remind you of one thing, though."

"And what's that?"

"A peaceful demonstration will help people to think about your message. A rowdy and unorganized one will create negativity and people won't listen. That's just something to think about."

Susan nodded. "I understand."

After unhitching his horse, William motioned for the rebellious women to follow him and they headed down the road to the sheriff's office. No one said a word as they followed him and he was grateful. As they came upon the school, he noticed that Laura was getting ready to climb into her buggy. When she saw them, her brow rose curiously.

Myrtle waved to her and called out, "Good afternoon, Miss McBride. We fought for our rights today, just as you suggested. And it feels mighty good. Now my husband will know I meant business."

When Laura gave him a questioning look, William shrugged, not sure what to say. He was arresting three women who were sticking up for their rights.

As he marched the women into the sheriff's office, he said, "This way, ladies."

William opened the jail cell and the women walked inside and sat down. After shutting the door and locking it, he turned around and saw a very surprised sheriff staring up at him.

"Do you want to tell me what this is about?" asked Nicholas as he pushed his paperwork aside.

Before he could answer, Myrtle said, "It's simple. We disobeyed the law, Nicholas. So he did his job."

The sheriff furrowed his brow and got to his feet. Sauntering to the jail cell, he said, "This doesn't look good, Myrtle. What's your husband going to say?"

"We'll find out, won't we?" she said with a grin. "I'm giving him a message. And this time he's going to listen."

Turning to William, he said, "Myrtle is the last person I thought I would ever see behind bars. I've never seen her give an opinion on anything. She's usually so quiet and reserved. I'm not sure what's come over her."

"Who is she?" asked William with great curiosity.

"She is Lawyer Randolph's wife, the most prominent and prestigious man in town."

William chuckled when he realized that Laura was making a difference in this community. That was probably why the women were taking a stand. He was amused when Myrtle called out to Laura, saying she had fought for her rights. She was giving Laura the credit for inspiring her to do so.

"What was the disturbance about down at Town Square?" asked Nicholas as he rubbed the stubble on his face.

"There's about two-dozen women standing in front of the Butcher's Shop. They're protesting his injustice. So I just told them to make sure it's a peaceful protest."

"Good job." As he took a seat at his desk, Nicholas said, "I want you to go to the post office to see if I received any replies from the lawmen I wrote to. I heard of some instances of thievery during revival meetings and asked for more details."

Giving a nod, William asked, "Do you need anything else?"

"Yes. Check out Town Square again and make sure all is well. Maybe stay and watch for a while."

Nicholas took some papers from his drawer that had the descriptions of men who were wanted for various crimes and carefully looked at each one.

William could see the stress on his face. It was Wednesday afternoon and Sam had not yet returned with the information. He knew the sheriff was on edge, just waiting to find out more about the thievery that had happened during the revival meetings. Since another revival was being planned in a week and a half, Nicholas wanted to be prepared.

When the sheriff came upon Frank McLaughlin's description, he sighed. Looking up at William, he said, "We need to look for this man. He may have left town but I suspect he'll be back."

"I understand," said William.

He remembered how quickly the man had gotten away from him, but he wouldn't let it happen again.

Looking up from his paperwork, Nicholas said, "Are you still here?"

William laughed and headed out the door to do his assignment.

As he pulled up to the post office, William was pleasantly surprised when he saw Laura's buggy outside the building. Dusting himself off and pushing his fingers through his hair, William walked inside the post office.

When he saw Laura standing in line waiting her turn, he walked up behind her and cleared his throat. "Good afternoon, Laura!"

When she turned around and saw him, her face lit up. "I'm mailing off a letter to my parents, letting them know how I'm doing. How about you?"

"The sheriff asked me to get the mail," he explained as he folded his arms over his chest. "How was your lecture at the school?"

Laura's eyes brightened as she said, "William, it was incredible. Those children were so receptive. I've got to tell you all about it. There was this one girl who…"

"Next!" said the postmaster.

Turning around, she handed her letter to him and paid for the postage. "Do I have any letters today?"

The postmaster checked her box and nodded. "You sure do, Miss McBride. It looks like you have two letters."

William raised his brow. "Two letters in one day? I'm lucky to get two in a month," he said jokingly.

Laura glanced at the names on the envelopes, gave a sigh and quickly stuffed the letters in her reticule.

For some reason, Laura looked as if something was bothering her. A person was usually happy or excited to get letters but she didn't seem excited.

"What's wrong?" he asked with concern.

She shook her head. "It's nothing."

"Are you sure?"

Laura nodded but the cheerful countenance in her face had left. There was definitely something bothering her.

When it was William's turn, he said, "Wait for me. I want to show you something."

With that said, he asked for the sheriff's mail. Since there was nothing, he followed her out the door.

"Are you on duty?" asked Laura.

He nodded. "I'm making my rounds, making sure Willow Valley is peaceful. I was just headed to Town Square. I would like to show you something. You can see the fruits of your labor."

"What do you mean?" she asked curiously.

William chuckled. "Follow me. You'll see what I mean. It may not be the quietest place to talk because there's a demonstration going on over there."

Tilting her head, she asked, "What kind of demonstration?"

"Apparently, one of the women applied for a job because her husband was injured. But the butcher wouldn't hire her, even though she has plenty of experience... because she's a woman. So her friends are doing a demonstration." He grinned. "And I'm sure it's because of you and your influence."

Laura's eyes widened. "Really? Are you serous?"

"Definitely. You're making a difference in this community."

She seemed speechless.

After tying his horse to the back of her buggy, William climbed in beside her and they took off toward Town Square.

When they pulled up to the park, William helped Laura down from the buggy. After tying the reins to a post, he held out his arm to her and she took it. Leading her to a bench, they sat down and watched the demonstration.

He noticed the women were not blocking the entrance but were holding their signs up high. Sally was speaking to a woman who was about to enter the Butcher's Shop. After hearing what she had to say, the woman turned around and left. Everything seemed under control.

With pride, William turned to her and said, "Do you see what you have created here, Miss McBride?"

"Wow! This is amazing," exclaimed Laura as she watched the women interact with shoppers. "I'm impressed."

When he slid his hand around her palm and intertwined their fingers, she looked up at him and smiled.

"Thank you, William. Thank you for bringing me here to see this."

As he looked at their hands clasped together, an overwhelming feeling of joy overtook William. His heart fluttered against his chest when she smiled at him. The feelings he had for this young woman were real and he wondered if she felt the same about him.

When Laura squeezed his hand in return, he wondered if it was because she was grateful or because she was as attracted to him as he was to her? Time would tell.

Chapter 7

It was Friday and Laura was pleasantly surprised to see how many people showed up at Town Square. The turnout was better than she had expected.

Standing under the gazebo, Laura scanned the audience and noticed they were ready. When she saw William standing at the back of the audience with his arms folded over his chest, Laura smiled. He was so supportive. Each time she saw the man, her heart would beat just a little faster. Her attraction for him was real.

He had told her that she was making a difference in Willow Valley, something she needed to hear. Each time she gave a lecture, she wondered if she was touching anyone's heart and whether they understood what she was saying. It was so nice to see the "fruits of her labor" as William had put it.

It was time to begin but she felt anxious, wondering if they would listen to her or scoff at her opinions. She was going to talk about a controversial subject. At that moment, William gave her a broad smile and slowly nodded his head. He was giving her the message that he was there to support her.

Stepping forward and holding a coin high above her head, she took a deep breath and was ready to begin. Speaking loud enough for everyone to hear, Laura said, "Do you see this coin in my hand? It says: Am I not a woman and a sister? She most certainly is. This woman is a child of God. She isn't any different than you or me."

When the women in the audience nodded in agreement, Laura smiled and breathed a little easier.

"I went to a lecture in Nantucket in 1841 and heard Frederick Douglass give a speech about freedom for all people. I had just turned eighteen at the time but it had a big impact on my life. He published his autobiography and told what it was like to live in slavery. I urge you to read it. To quote Mr. Douglass: *All the American people need is light.* He said if we knew the truth, we would fight against such abominations."

With that said, the women nodded and voiced their opinions, agreeing with her. Laura felt pleased with their reaction. But a few men at the back shook their heads. Sadly, they didn't agree with her.

Standing boldly before her audience, she said, "Involuntary servitude is wrong. We must fight against such laws and let our voice be heard. I encourage you to boycott all the products produced from slave labor. Only buy from the free Northern States! Most cotton for your clothes and sugar come from the South, but we will not relent. Our voices will be heard."

"You don't know what you're talking about, lady," yelled a Southern gentleman at the back of the audience. "Go home and tend to your house… for that's what women do best."

A gruff-looking man stepped forward and yelled, "You don't understand what you're expecting of us. If no one buys from us, we'll lose everything. We'll lose our crops. We'll go bankrupt. You're talking about a subject you don't know nothin' about."

A businessman in a suit raised his fist in the air and yelled, "It's improper for a lady to preach publicly. It's unwomanly and unchristian. Go home, lady!"

"I don't mind being told I'm unwomanly," Laura said with spunk. "But I'm going to defend my faith. I'm a devout Christian. And I believe what I'm doing is what God wants me to do. How about you? Does God want you to take away people's agency?"

The man did not answer but furrowed his brow and mumbled something that she did not understand.

Taking a deep breath, she held up the coin once again and looked into the eyes of the women. "Am I not a woman and a sister? I assure you this woman is a child of God." Then staring at the men at the back of the audience, she continued. "Servitude against one's will is unchristian. You can't convince me otherwise."

With that statement, the men bristled. The gruff-looking man began yelling at her and cursing. He looked as if he were ready to tar and feather her. His eyes and attitude were frightening. The rest of the men followed suit and called out their complaints, as well. What she had just said was not taken well.

Realizing things were getting out of hand, William quickly used his authority as a deputy and told the men to leave. She could see they were reluctant to go and began to argue with him. So William picked a man up by his collar and trousers then hoisted him out of Town Square. When he returned, the rest of the men realized he meant business. For fear of being arrested, they reluctantly gave in and left.

Turning to Laura, William called out to her from the back of the audience, "I sent them away for their own good. I hated to see what would have happened if all these women had gotten to them first."

With that announcement, the women broke into laughter. Feeling encouraged, Laura continued her speech.

Afterward, the women complimented her and said they would spread the word about buying from the Northern States only.

When everyone had left, William walked up to her and said, "Well done, Miss McBride. That was an impressive speech."

With gratitude, she said warmly, "Thank you for your help, William. I wasn't ready for such a disruption."

"Did you have any idea that you would get that sort of reaction to your speech?"

She shook her head. "I guess I shouldn't have accused them of being unchristian. They didn't take it well. Although, that's exactly how I felt."

William nodded his understanding. "Maybe I should see you home... just in case you meet an undesirable person who attended your lecture."

Holding his arm out to her, she smiled at his concern and took it.

"By the way," said William as they walked toward her buggy. "You're the most womanly woman I know. Don't believe a word that man said."

Tilting her head curiously, she asked, "Is that so?"

He winked at her. "Of course. Today, as you spoke to your audience and told those men off, your righteous indignation made me so proud of you."

Laura couldn't help but smile at his words. Holding onto his arm, she remembered how he had lifted the belligerent man up and hoisted him out of Town Square. The joy she felt as she watched him was overwhelming. After seeing what had happened to their comrade, all the hecklers quickly left. William was her hero.

After making sure she arrived home safely, Laura stood at the front door and said, "I'm glad that you attended my lecture today. If you hadn't been there, I don't know what I would have done."

William folded his arms across his chest and smiled. "I'm glad I attended. Next time, don't accuse the guilty parties of being unchristian. They didn't take lightly to it."

She laughed and gave a firm nod. "I'll take your advice. I want to make a difference. Not cause a riot."

"Are you going to the dance tomorrow night?"

"Of course. Dancing is my favorite pastime."

"Save a dance for me?"

With a coy smile, she opened the door and said, "Perhaps. We'll see."

With that said, she closed the door behind her.

* * *

As William climbed into his saddle, he realized he was falling for Laura. There was no doubt about it. She was such a spunky young lady who wasn't afraid to speak on a controversial subject. It took bravery to speak on women's rights and freedom for all. Being an activist and abolitionist was not easy, especially if you were a woman preaching about it.

Since she spoke out on such controversial subjects, William hoped she wouldn't experience the same thing that happened to Mary. He would have to watch her carefully.

After arriving at the sheriff's office, he tied his horse to a hitching post next to a water barrel. He smoothed his hand over his mane and allowed him to drink.

Nicholas walked outside onto the porch and sat down on a rocking chair. As he rocked back and forth, he said, "How did the lecture turn out? Any problems?"

William raised his brow as he pointed to the chair. "Where did that come from?"

Nicholas grinned as he gently rocked back and forth. "My wife says I have too much anxiety because of these revivals. So she brought this over and told me to sit in it for an hour every time I feel stressed. The rocking motion is supposed to relax me."

William chuckled. "Is it working?"

The sheriff shrugged his shoulders. "We'll see. So tell me about the lecture."

"It went well. Although I was a little worried. It almost got out of hand."

Folding his arms over his chest, Nicholas leaned back and continued rocking. "What happened? Tell me about it."

Stepping onto the porch, he sat down on a bench. A smile played at the corners of his lips as he remembered her spunky speech. "Laura encouraged everyone to boycott products produced in the South from plantation owners. Then she called a bunch of hecklers unchristian. They didn't take kindly to it. So I had to boot them out of Town Square."

"You like her, don't you?" accused Nicholas with a teasing glint in his eyes. "Admit it. You like her. I can tell."

William nodded. "Yes, I do. She's so different from other women. She's not afraid to say what's on her mind if she feels there's injustice in the world. She's brave and feminine. Yes, I really like her."

"Did you invite her to the dance tomorrow night?"

William grinned. "I sure did. And every time I asked her to save me a dance, she was so elusive. She kept saying: Perhaps. We'll see."

Nicholas chuckled. "They have the best music and refreshments." Giving a sigh, he said, "Well, I hate to change the subject, but Sam came in today with some news."

William leaned back, waiting to hear what he had found out. The sheriff had been on edge, just waiting to find out if his assumptions were correct.

Nicholas continued rocking and shook his head. "It isn't good news."

"What did Sam find out?"

"According to the sheriff in Memphis, there have been quite a few thefts during revival meetings. Sheriff Carter feels the infamous Wages and Copeland Gang are involved. If so, they are a ruthless bunch who don't blink an eye when it comes to killing anyone who gets in their way." Nicholas groaned. "Sheriff Carter said he suspects Frank McLaughlin belongs to that gang."

Neither Nicholas nor William had expected that kind of news. He figured there was a no-good horse thief to catch. But Frank was not alone. He was part of a gang, which brought up one question. How many were in Willow Valley?

"In other words, Willow Valley is in trouble," concluded William.

"That's right. In a week, the revivals begin again. I'm going to ask the militia to help us."

William was quiet and didn't know what to say. Including the Willow Valley Militia would be perfect. They needed more than the sheriff and a deputy to stop the Wages and Copeland Gang. Willow Valley was usually a quiet place. William never suspected something like this.

Pulling his watch from his vest, he checked the time. His work was done and it was time to relax. "I'm in the mood for some hot chocolate. Want some?"

Nicholas shook his head as he rocked back and forth. "I'll see you tomorrow. I'm heading home soon."

Climbing onto his horse, William headed to Hannah's Hot Chocolate Shoppe. Her chocolate drink always cheered him up. He needed something. The idea that a notorious gang might be arriving in Willow Valley in one week unnerved him.

After tying his horse to a post, he walked into the shop and said, "Hot chocolate, please!"

As he placed some coins on the counter, Hannah said, "Are you all right, William? You look like you've lost your best friend."

He tried to look cheerful but didn't quite feel it. "It's just been a stressful day. So I figured some hot chocolate would do the job."

As she poured some into a cup, William's eyes brightened when Laura just happened to walk into the shop. With a raise of his brow, he asked, "You, too?"

Laura nodded. "I thought it would take away my stress. After my lecture today, I had a tough time relaxing. I've never had that sort of disturbance before. Elizabeth Stanton told me that I would have days like this." Placing some coins on the counter, she said, "Hot chocolate, please."

As William took his cup and sat down at a table, he said, "Sit with me and we can cheer each other up."

Tilting her head curiously, she asked, "What's wrong?"

He took a sip of chocolate and gave a shrug of his shoulders. He was not sure whether it was a good idea to tell her that a gang could be responsible for the thievery in town... and they just might be returning.

Taking her cup, she sat down across from William and said, "I'm ready. Tell me about it."

William wondered if it was wise to tell her about his concerns, but he had to get it off his chest. He needed to talk to someone.

Placing his cup on the table, he said, "We just got word that the man you found in your house might be part of a gang."

When her eyes widened, William was glad he hadn't mentioned that the Copeland Gang was known as one of the most notorious gangs this side of the Mississippi.

"What are they doing here?" asked Laura.

"We learned that revivals are drawing them. They take advantage of thousands of people gathering together and steal from them."

"Oh no." She shook her head with dismay. "What are you going to do?"

"If we can find the man who snuck into your home, he'll lead us to the others."

Laura sipped her chocolate then placed her mug on the table. "I sense there's something else bothering you, William. What is it?"

He smiled at her intuition and gave a deep sigh. "I haven't been a deputy long. This is new to me and I'm feeling anxious. I'm afraid I'll disappoint the sheriff. I was part of the Willow Valley Militia before this assignment, so I'm not a stranger to keeping the peace. But this is totally different. It makes me uneasy."

"But that's good, William. Don't you see? If you were feeling confident, you could make a mistake. Being anxious will keep you on your toes."

William knew she was trying to make him feel better. It didn't. But it touched his heart that she was trying. "Thank you. I'll remember that." Leaning toward her with great interest, he said, "Now it's your turn. I'm curious. What do your parents think about your crusade? Are they worried about your safety? Do they support you?"

"Oh! What do my parents think?" she said with laughter. "That's a loaded question. They believe in my cause. And they're all for Elizabeth Stanton giving speeches about women's rights.

They think it's wonderful. But they're worried about me. They're afraid of the consequences."

"You're their daughter and they want to protect you. It's only natural."

Laura sighed. "I know."

"At least they believe in your cause. Because of you and women like you, eventually women will have the right to vote. And freedom will be given to all men and women. You just wait and see."

She placed her hand on his and smiled. "Thank you for your support."

William glanced down at her hand and grinned. "As long as we have men and women fighting against prejudice, it will happen. I'm sure of it."

Chapter 8

Saturday night William headed for the town social in his finest clothes, hoping to see Laura once again. She really sparked an interest in him, and he couldn't get her off his mind.

As he walked into the building, he could hear the lively music playing. Some people were dancing and others were standing around the refreshment table. When William scanned the room, he saw Laura dancing the gallopade. Her dark ringlets framed her face, accentuating her beauty, and her sky blue eyes brightened when she laughed.

As William watched her graceful movements, he thought of her dynamic speech that she gave about women's rights. She had such poise and dignity. Her attitude was one of confidence, as if she knew women would vote one day. Laura McBride definitely intrigued him.

When the dance came to an end, he walked toward her with the intention of asking her for a dance but he was not quick enough. No sooner had she left the dance floor that a gentleman took her by the hand and guided her back.

Remembering he was there to dance, as well, William found another partner and joined in the dancing.

Throughout the evening, he did not have a chance to dance with Laura because someone would beat him to it every time. But he had a plan. The next time the music stopped, he would not wait until she was escorted off the floor.

When the music came to an end, William briskly walked toward her with determination. Apparently another gentleman had the same idea and butted in front of him, blocking his way. The man was rude but William couldn't do anything about it without making a scene.

With a broad smile and a bow, the gentleman said, "May I have this dance, Miss McBride?"

Feeling dejected, William was about to turn around and leave the dance floor when he heard Laura's answer.

"I can't. I'm sorry. I promised this dance to Deputy Davies."

When William noticed that she was holding her hand out towards him, he smiled.

"Shall we dance?" Laura asked with her usual coy smile. "I did promise to save you a dance, didn't I?"

William chuckled. "As I remember, you said... perhaps. You wouldn't commit."

Laura laughed as he approached her.

"The Virginia Reel," announced the music director. "Grab your partner!"

A Mississippi Sunset

As they took their place across from each other, Laura's eyes brightened. "This is one of my favorite dances."

It didn't take long until the dancers formed two lines down the middle of the floor, with the gentlemen on one side and the ladies on the other. Without hesitation, the music began.

William had such fun, weaving between the couples, then back to his partner again. As he took her by the waist, he promenaded her to the head of the line. When he sashayed around her, he grinned and winked at her, letting her know he was having a grand time.

When the music finally stopped, William asked, "Would you like something to drink?"

She nodded. "Oh yes. I'm thirsty."

He took her hand and guided her toward the refreshment table. "You are a fine dancer. Where did you learn to dance so well?"

"At the Troy Seminary." Tilting her head curiously, Laura said, "Every time we get together, you always ask questions about me. It's my turn. I'd like to know something about you."

As he poured her a drink, William said, "Certainly. What would you like to know?"

"You mentioned that you're from Wales. Was it hard to adjust when you first arrived here?"

William thought about it, and there was a period of adjustment. Handing her the cup, he said, "It was a bit stressful at first because everything was so different, like the language, food, and customs. But I was excited to experience something new and different. As for my sister, she was homesick at first because our parents are still in Wales. I've heard others mention they felt lost at times. When I think about it, I don't regret moving here. I'm quite happy and satisfied with my life."

Laura nodded. "I'm glad."

"How about you? Are you enjoying Willow Valley? It's quite a change from the big city."

She took a sip of her drink and nodded. "Yes, it's very different, but I like it. I'm getting more and more opportunities to give speeches, much more than I had in New York. There was too much opposition there. Of course, there will always be those who will stubbornly oppose it."

Shaking his head, William said, "I don't understand why you're getting opposition."

Laura gave a deep sigh. "Some people don't like change. I've read a few articles that say women don't have the mental capacity to understand politics. So there's no need to have them vote."

"Balderdash!" exclaimed William. "I don't believe it."

His sister was one of the smartest women he knew. She had an education and had more sense than the average man. Of course, he wouldn't admit that in front of her. She was too much fun to tease.

With conviction, William said, "My father said women have a very important role in this life, because they teach future generations. Not men... but women. And it takes a lot of know-how and intelligence to raise a family. As for equality? My sister demands respect and she gets it, too."

With a gentle smile, Laura took his hand and said, "Enough about politics. Let's have fun. They're playing the Boston Waltz. Shall we dance?"

William glanced around the room as he said hesitantly, "Depends. Is Preacher Armstrong anywhere in sight?"

Raising her brow, she asked, "Why?"

"Have you heard his sermon on dancing the waltz recently?"

She laughed. "Yes, I have. I heard it first hand. He said it was wanton behavior. I just said I would take his advice into consideration." Tilting her head curiously, she asked, "Are you ready?"

He nodded eagerly. "I sure am."

"Good. Let's do it."

With a broad grin, William followed her onto the dance floor.

As he glanced around the room, he was surprised to see Nicholas and his wife standing right in the center of the room, ready to dance the waltz.

He noticed there weren't as many on the dance floor. It was probably because of Armstrong's preaching. He may have put the fear of God in their hearts. Personally, he believed that God was just fine with the waltz. There wasn't anything wrong with it.

Before long, the music began. Taking Laura into his arms, they danced across the floor. The Boston Waltz was slower paced that the waltzes in England and Wales, but he liked it just fine.

Looking down at Laura, he realized that holding her in his arms was the perfect way to end the evening. She was an excellent dancer and fit in his arms perfectly. Deep down inside, he knew his attraction for Laura was growing daily.

* * *

The following day Laura sat on her porch swing, thinking about the enjoyable evening she had at the town social. William was such an entertaining fellow. She really liked him. He believed in her crusade, hoping to change the world.

Just then Mary pulled up to the house with her eight year old son, Mark. After helping her son down from the buggy, they headed to the porch with a gift in her hand.

"I have some fresh bread for you," announced Mary cheerfully. "I thought you could use a little cheering up."

Laura smiled at her friend's comment. "How did you know?"

"Emmeline told me what happened at church today. She said you looked discouraged."

Laura nodded. "Our pastor made an announcement that I didn't expect. I don't blame him, though. He's worried about his congregation because it's becoming divided. There's bickering and arguments."

"That was what Emmeline told me. But it isn't just his congregation, Laura. People have their opinions about equality and let it be known."

"I know," said Laura with a sigh. "He said when the government is ready to make a change, it will happen. In the meantime, be patient and obey the laws of the land."

With a mischievous grin, Mary said, "But... my father said the squeaky wheel always gets attention."

Laura broke into laughter. "In other words, I should be a squeaky wheel?"

"Of course!"

When she saw Mark watching her, Laura smiled at the young boy. He was so shy. Recently he began speaking to her, and she was happy that he had accepted her as a friend.

"How are you this fine day, young man?"

A light smattering of freckles covered his nose and cheeks, and his wavy auburn hair was unruly. When he smiled, his eyes lit up as he replied, "I'm fine. Did you know I can make my cat eat a radish?"

"No, I didn't know that."

"I can make him eat a pickle, too."

With a raise of her brow, Laura said, "You can? I didn't know cats loved radishes and pickles. I'd have to see it to believe it."

"Do you have a cat?"

She shook her head. "Unfortunately, I don't."

"If you did, I could show you."

Laura laughed at his eagerness. "Maybe when I stop by to visit, you can show me."

With a teasing glint in her eyes, Mary said, "I know something you probably don't know." She shrugged her shoulders. "Or maybe you just might know."

"And what's that?" she asked with humor in her voice.

"I know a certain deputy who really likes you. I haven't seen him pay this much attention to anyone before."

Laura nodded. "I suspected as much. He's so sweet. But I don't have time for relationships. I'm on a crusade and you know that. Besides, he's just a friend."

In a sober tone, Mary said, "All you need is a man who will support you, and you can do anything your heart desires." She placed her hands on her hips and gave a firm nod. "I think you should invite him over for supper. That way you can get to know each other better. Besides, I think he needs a little encouragement."

Tilting her head curiously, Laura asked, "Encouragement? What do you mean by that?"

"After the way you treated him each time he asked you to save him a dance?" She cleared her throat and shook her head. "I think he needs a little encouragement."

With laughter, Laura said, "I was teasing him. Besides, we're just friends."

"I know. I know," said Mary as if she didn't believe her.

"I don't want to encourage him. Besides…"

At that point, Laura stopped. There was much more that she hadn't revealed to her dear friend and she wasn't sure if she wanted to tell her or not.

Creasing her brow, Mary said, "Besides what? Don't you want to find out more about him… get to know him better? He really likes you. How about the time when he stopped those rabble-rousers from causing trouble down at Town Square? He booted them out unceremoniously, didn't he?"

Laura smiled, remembering how gallant he was that day. "But that's different. It was his duty as a deputy to keep the peace."

"Was it his duty to take you home afterwards?"

"He didn't want anyone following me so he was protecting me. It was his duty as a…"

"I know. I know," said Mary with laughter. "It was his duty as a deputy. Listen to yourself. You're trying to talk yourself out of getting to know him. My dearest friend, listen to me. If you don't give him a chance…"

"We're just friends," interrupted Laura with urgency.

Mary gazed into her eyes and raised her brow curiously. "There's something bothering you. I can tell. What is it?"

Laura sighed. "I'm promised to someone else. That's what's bothering me. I have to respect my parents' wishes, as well. And that's bothering me. Besides that, I'm attracted to William when I shouldn't be. So that's bothering me."

Mary frowned. "There's more, isn't there?"

Laura nodded and decided to tell her friend everything. "Our parents are good friends so they arranged it. According to my parents, he's been interested in me for quite some time. So they thought it was a good match."

"Are you serious? They actually arranged it?"

"I was attending an all female school," said Laura, hoping to explain her dilemma. "And I only give speeches to women's groups. My parents were concerned so they thought I needed some help."

"Are you engaged?"

"No. Not yet."

"Do you love him?"

Laura shrugged her shoulders. "I haven't seen Albert for a few years because he's been attending college in Massachusetts, but he writes to me every so often. Although, every time I get a letter from him, I feel guilty because I'm attracted to William."

"I see."

"He's planning to come out here to court me, so we can get to know one another better."

"So you're not engaged and you're not in love with him," said Mary with a sigh of relief. "Good. As I see it, there's nothing wrong with seeing other men. Especially when William is *just* a friend. Am I not right? Besides, you don't want to marry the wrong man. What if Albert isn't meant for you? What if he doesn't support your cause? What if he's disagreeable? You don't want to regret your decision. I know you want to respect your parents' wishes, but marriage is something you mustn't take lightly."

Her friend was right. She wasn't engaged to Albert, as of yet. Even though she had been promised to him, Laura needed to choose the man who was meant for her. What worried her most was how her parents would react.

Pulling a card from her bag, Mary said, "I made this for you. It's an invitation for William." She handed it to Laura. "All you have to do is add a date and time and then sign it."

With amusement, Laura asked, "Are you serious?"

Mary grinned and gave a nod. "Of course. Invite him over for supper. I'm going to pass by his place on the way home, so I'll wait until you fill it out and I'll take it to him."

With a raise of her brow, Laura asked, "Do you live close to him?"

"Just a few miles south. Mark and I were going for a little Sunday ride today, so we can drop it by."

Laura laughed as she got up and went into the house. Mary was willing to go the extra mile to make sure he got this invitation. She was so persistent. After penning tomorrow's date and time, she signed it. There was no need to put it off for a few days.

Pushing the front door open, she marched outside and handed it to Mary. "All right! Since this is your idea, what do you suggest I serve him?"

Getting to her feet, Mary said, "I did my part in getting you two together. The rest is up to you." She turned to her son and grinned. "Let's go, Mark. We have an invitation to deliver."

Laura bit her lip as she watched her dear friend walk to her buggy. Now she had to figure out what to serve her guest.

Chapter 9

The following day Laura put together a menu that she hoped William would like. It was time to find out what kind of person he was. Laura knew that her parents were concerned with her crusade because of the opposing forces. But they supported her, anyway. How would William feel about it if she were more than a friend?

While the roast beef and potatoes were cooking in the oven, she cleaned the house and made sure it was in order. Then she headed for her room to get ready.

After making a loose bun at the back of her head, she took some bandoline, dipped her fingers into the clear liquid and created small ringlets at the side of her face. It took a little while for the curls to set but she was pleased with the outcome.

Choosing a flowered gown, she pulled it on and looked in the mirror. As she turned around and looked at every angle, Laura felt pleased. It was gathered below the bodice and just above her hips, complementing her figure. Laura smoothed her hand over her skirt then headed downstairs. Looking at the clock in the front room, she realized it was past time for William to arrive. He was ten minutes late.

Taking the roast and potatoes from the oven, she placed them on a platter. When she heard a knock at the door, she froze. It had been a while since she had entertained a guest and felt nervous. Laura had to tell her beating heart to be still. William was just a friend and she was only doing this as a favor to Mary.

Glancing in the mirror, she checked her hair and then opened the door. There stood William looking so dapper in his green pinstriped vest and white cravat about his neck. He was looking at his pocket watch when she opened the door. Placing it in his vest, he looked up and smiled.

"Sorry I'm late. As I passed the town clock, I realized my watch was slow. I was just setting it."

Pushing his fingers through his dark brown hair, he grinned. His charming smile created small dimples in his cheeks and his chocolate brown eyes asked her to forgive his tardiness.

"Don't worry. It's not a problem," she said as she motioned for him to enter. "I just took the roast out of the oven. So you're just in time."

Smelling the aroma that wafted toward them, he said, "Mmm, roast beef. It smells good."

"Follow me, please," said Laura as she guided him to the next room.

She led him to a dining room with a red brick fireplace. Since she was having a guest, Laura chose her best dining ware. Excusing herself, she went to the kitchen and brought out the platter of food.

As Laura placed it on the table, she noticed William lighting the candles of her candelabrum. Then he placed it in the center of the table and pulled a chair out for her to be seated.

As he took a seat across from her, she motioned to the candles and said, "Thank you, William. I appreciate your help."

He gave a nod. "You're welcome."

After saying a prayer on the food, she passed him the platter.

"You look lovely this evening," said William as he dished some roast beef onto his plate.

"Why, thank you, William," she said, giving him the usual coy smile.

Her beating heart told her that he was someone special but her mind told her to be cautious and to take this relationship slow.

As they ate, William told her a little about his parents and what it was like growing up in Wales.

With a half smile playing at the corners of his lips, he said, "As a boy, I did many foolish things and soon found that my mother would not endure such foolishness. She was very sober and serious-minded. Even though she was strict, she was charitable and generous to those in need. She was kind-hearted to everyone she met, to the pauper and even a fallen woman who needed sympathy."

With great interest, Laura asked, "How about your father? What was he like?"

"He was a religious man and had great faith in God. Whenever my sisters wanted anything, they went to him instead of Mother because they usually got it." He chuckled. "If Mother thought it was a foolish pleasure, she would say to him: John, you shouldn't encourage such a thing. Then he would plead: Oh, let the little maid have it, dear."

With that, Laura broke into laughter. "I love your father all ready."

William grinned. "How about you? Were your parents strict? Did they make sure you learned needlework and how to cook?" He pointed to his plate. "Such as this delicious meal?"

She laughed. "Of course. But I had a mind of my own. I was very active and enjoyed being outside. I climbed trees with my older brothers, jumped in a creek when I was hot, ripped my skirts in the process, and got into trouble several times. My parents worried that I would never settle down and act like a young lady."

"Is that so?" William said with humor in his voice.

"That's right. My mother usually listened to my needs but Father was more stubborn. He was strict and wanted me to get a proper education at a boarding school, hoping I would settle down and learn some etiquette. Little did he know what he had done by sending me there! That was when my eyes were truly opened. I soon realized that I wanted to fight for women's rights, but my friends thought I was crazy."

A Mississippi Sunset

"I don't think so," said William adamantly. "It's about time someone spoke out for women. My father always said that women see a different side of things. When a decision has to be made, my parents always discussed it. That's what a proper marriage should be like... two intelligent people making a decision together."

What he said touched her heart. His father was very wise. That was an example of what a married couple should be like. She liked the idea of two intelligent people making a decision together.

When William placed his hand on hers and gently squeezed her fingers, warmth crept up her arm and went straight to her heart. She swallowed and tried to tell her beating heart to slow down. Realizing he was having an effect on her, she quickly changed the subject.

Pulling her hand free, she cleared her throat. "How is the roast beef? Is it to your liking?"

He took another bite and smiled. "Mm hm. This is so tender and juicy. What's your secret?"

Tilting her head curiously, she asked, "My secret?"

"Every time I make roast beef, it's always dry. My sister says I cook it way too long and that's my problem."

With stunned surprise, Laura asked, "Are you telling me that you don't expect your sister to wait on you and do all the cooking?"

William shook his head. "Of course not. Serenity teaches a class in the evening three times a week so I help out on those nights. At first I didn't, though. I thought it was a woman's responsibility. I was adamant that men had their chores. And I wouldn't budge."

With stunned surprise, Laura said, "So what changed your mind?"

"I was talking to Mary one day, and she told me that men should help out with chores and to not expect to be waited upon. So I asked her why that was important because women have their chores to do and so do men."

"What was her answer?"

"If a man wasn't willing to help out, then he was selfish and uncaring. Why would a woman want to be with her husband in the hereafter if he didn't help her right here on earth?" He chuckled. "That was an idea that I hadn't thought about. After that, I decided to help out. I even beat the rugs when it's needed."

Laura smiled and said softly, "Therein lies the secret to a happy marriage."

He nodded. "That's exactly what she said."

Having William over for supper was a wonderful idea because she was getting to know him so much better.

After taking a sip of his herbal tea, he asked, "So what's your secret?"

"I always top it with plenty of rosemary and salt. Then I add just a little water and cover it with a lid. Most people don't think of that, but I feel it makes the beef more tender and moist. Try it next time."

Setting her cup down, Laura rolled her shoulders to relax her sore muscles.

A Mississippi Sunset

As she rubbed her lower back with her knuckles, William cocked his head and asked, "Are you all right?"

She laughed. "I did some weeding this morning and was out longer than I intended. I probably overdid a little. But I'll be fine after a good night's sleep."

William nodded as he gathered their plates, utensils, and cups together. Then he headed to the kitchen with the stack of dishes in his hands, which surprised her greatly. Quickly, she grabbed hold of the platter and followed him into the kitchen.

When she saw him pouring hot water from the kettle into a dishpan, she asked curiously, "What are you doing?"

He glanced over his shoulder and shrugged. "You were on your feet for quite a while making a delicious meal. I'd like to help. Sit down and relax," he said as he searched her cupboards. "Where are the soap flakes?"

Shaking her head, she said, "You don't have to do this."

"But I want to." When he found the flakes, he grinned. "Ah-ha! Here it is."

Taking the box, he sprinkled some flakes into the water then placed the plates in the water and began scrubbing them clean.

She was amazed. Apparently, his talk with Mary had influenced him a great deal. As she sat down and watched him work, Laura wondered if Albert, the man she was supposed to marry, would even care that her muscles were sore. Her parents thought Albert was the perfect match. But was he really?

After William placed the last of the dishes in the drainer, he took a small towel and dried his hands. With a raise of his brow, he asked, "Would you be interested in attending a horserace with me tomorrow evening? It's quite entertaining. What do you think?"

His offer took her completely off guard. Usually a suitor took her to a concert, recital, or play. This would be a totally different experience.

With a nod, she said eagerly, "I would love to go. What time should I be ready?"

William's eyes brightened as he said, "It starts at seven o'clock. So I'll pick you up at six thirty."

She walked him to the door, excited to see him again. As they walked onto the porch, Laura noticed the sun had just gone down. There were all shades of orange and pink on the horizon, blending into the wispy clouds above.

William stared at the gorgeous sunset for a few seconds and then turned to her. "I had a nice time tonight. And the meal was delicious."

"Thank you, William. You are quite the conversationalist."

"I try to be." Leaning his back against the porch railing, he cocked his head curiously. "Why did you invite me over tonight?"

"What do you mean?"

He folded his arms over his chest in a business like manner. "Every time I asked you to save me a dance, you wouldn't commit. I wasn't sure where I stood with you."

Laura stepped next to him and placed her hand on the railing. "I guess I shouldn't have teased you like that. Sorry."

His lips tugged at the corners as if trying to hold back a smile. Taking her hand in his, he said, "You were merciless. No compassion for an immigrant. You should have empathy for me. I'm trying to get used to your American customs."

She laughed at his playfulness and was about to give him a retort when he brought her fingers to his lips, giving them a tender kiss. Instantly warmth crept up her arm and engulfed her. Why was she drawn to this man? What was it about him that made her heart beat just a little quicker?

When his eyes softened, she instantly sensed the shift in his mood. The way he was looking down at Laura warmed her heart. As William touched her cheek, her heart beat almost out of control. He was so affectionate. Not able to resist, she stepped closer and looked up at his handsome face. She was drawn to him without a doubt. With a tender smile, William pulled her into his arms.

Just then Preacher Armstrong walked out onto his porch and cleared his throat rather loudly. Without hesitation, she instantly pulled away from William and backed up. When her face felt warm to the touch, she knew she was blushing. Had the preacher been peering out his window at them? Was he making sure she was safe since her parents weren't home to protect her?

With a chuckle, William said, "Well, I guess I'd better go. Thank you for a lovely evening, Laura." Taking her hand in his, he grinned. "See you tomorrow."

As he kissed her hand, she felt her knees become weak. Laura could not deny the fact that she was enjoying his affections.

With that, he walked down the steps of the porch and headed for his horse.

Laura tried to still her beating heart but it wouldn't slow down. William had definitely wedged his way into her heart and she knew it would be hard to get him off her mind.

Chapter 10

"I'm falling in love with Laura," announced William with conviction.

His statement had taken his sister by surprise, so much so that she dropped her spoon in the chowder that she was cooking for their noonday meal.

Turning to him, Serenity asked, "What did you say?"

"You heard me."

With doubt in her voice, she said, "You haven't known her that long. It's impossible to fall in love in such a short time."

"For the past month, I've attended her lectures. I've gotten to know her."

"Listening to lectures is not good enough. I think you're just infatuated with her."

He shook his head. "It's not infatuation." Stepping toward her, he placed his hands on her shoulders and looked into her eyes. "My mind tells me that she is good for me, and my heart tells me that I'm smitten with her. How do I ignore my heart and mind? Can you tell me that?"

Serenity shrugged. "I just worry that you'll get hurt."

"Each time I attended one of her lectures, I wished I could get to know her better. It wasn't until she walked into the sheriff's office that I had the opportunity of meeting her. Every time we're together, I'm so happy. Really! It's the truth."

She frowned as she shook her head. "But William, the two of you are so different. She's strong-minded and very independent. You're rather laid back and want to settle down. She's an activist and you're rather conservative. She's an American and you're Welsh. Do you have anything in common at all?"

He grinned. "Actually, that's what makes it so exciting to be around her."

"Just take it slow," she begged. "Marriage is a big step and you want to be sure of what you're doing."

He smiled at her concern and gave a nod. "I'm taking her to the horserace tomorrow."

"You are?" she said with stunned surprise. "That's not the average place to take a young lady if you're courting her. It's not that romantic, if you know what I mean. Should I teach you how to court a young lady?"

He laughed. "Laura accepted."

"She did?" said Serenity with a raised brow. "Really?"

William nodded. "It's going to be fun."

* * *

The racetrack was a huge field. Spectators stood on the sides to watch while others chose the elevated platforms to stand on. Those who wanted to have a far better view used binoculars.

Laura watched the people as they gathered together, talking excitedly about the race. As the spectators passed by, she heard them talking excitedly about a horse named Duchess. Apparently, she was an outstanding horse.

Taking Laura's hand, William led her to one of the platforms. She looked down at the horses standing together at the starting line, waiting for the race to begin.

Curiously, she asked, "Is there a certain horse that you're cheering for, William?"

He grinned. "Duchess. She's the white horse and the rider is wearing a purple jacket and hat." Handing her some binoculars, he said, "You'll be able to see better with these, especially when they get a ways off. Do you see those hedges and fences?"

She nodded.

"Each horse is supposed to jump over them. And at the far end of the field near that group of trees is a stream of water that they're supposed to leap over. This isn't only how fast your horse can run but how well trained it is."

Laura nodded her understanding.

When the sheriff walked out to the starting line, he held up his pistol and waited until he got everyone's attention. When he pulled the trigger, the horses took off.

As Duchess passed by, William called out, as he raised both arms in the air, "Woo-hoo! Way to go, Duchess! Move your blooomin' rump!"

Laura's eyes widened when she heard William.

He glanced at her and grinned. "Sorry. I tend to get excited at these races." Pointing to the rider in purple, he said, "That's my sister. She trained Duchess herself."

With stunned surprise, she stared at Duchess and its rider. Women were not allowed to enter a man's sport. Quickly putting the binoculars to her eyes, she watched as Duchess flew over one hedge after another. Next was a fence for the horses to jump over. Some tripped the top bar and it fell to the ground. But Duchess flew over it with ease.

At the end of the field was a stream full of water. A few horses came to a sudden halt and the riders went flying into the water. Others slowed down and carefully walked to the other side. Laura held her breath. Would Duchess make it? The anticipation was exciting as she watched Duchess speed up and fly over the stream with ease.

Laura jumped in the air and clapped her hands as she hollered, "Way to go, Duchess! Way to go!"

As each of the horses sped to the finish line, it was no surprise to Laura that Duchess won the race.

Without hesitation, she clapped her hands and cheered along with the crowd. It never occurred to her that she would enjoy such a sport. The enthusiasm of the audience and the excitement of cheering for a rider were quite enjoyable.

Turning to her, William asked, "Did you enjoy it?"

"Of course!" With a tilt of her head, she asked, "When your sister told you that she wanted to enter the race, what was your response? I'm curious."

He chuckled. "I was against it at first and tried to talk her out of it. Men's sports can get quite rambunctious and I was worried she might get hurt. Usually men put aside all gentlemanly manners in a race. When Serenity is determined to do something, no one can stop her. So I decided to support her, instead."

Laura was impressed with his attitude. He was one of a kind. She had never met a man such as this before.

As they stepped down from the platform, a distinguished gentleman walked up to her and said in a stern tone, "I would like to speak to you, Miss McBride."

Stepping aside so they were not in the way of traffic, she asked, "What is on your mind, sir?"

He furrowed his brow. "My wife and I were happy the way things were in our marriage until you came to town. I don't appreciate your interference. You had better watch what you say in public meetings from now on." Turning to

William, he growled, "And that goes for your sister, too. She had better keep out of my way."

Laura was speechless and wasn't sure what to say. Before she could get her senses about her, the man marched away.

William slipped his hand around hers and said, "That was Lawyer Randolph. It was his wife that was arrested when she stood up for women's rights. She told us that you were her inspiration. The fine to get her out of jail was quite substantial. I can tell you that much."

"Really?" Raising her brow curiously, she asked, "What did he mean that your sister had better keep out of his way?"

William chuckled. "Lawyer Randolph's horse is a fast runner and he has won every race. That is, until Serenity came along. He's not very happy about it and feels that women shouldn't be allowed to enter a man's sport. But Nicholas said there was nothing wrong with it and allowed her to enter." Motioning to his sister, William asked, "Would you like to meet her?"

Not able to resist, she rose on her toes and kissed his cheek.

With a smile playing at the corners of his lips, he said, "I assume that meant yes."

She nodded. But that wasn't the reason she had kissed his cheek. It was obvious that he believed in her cause and she couldn't resist.

After a short visit with Serenity, he took her for a drive to the Mississippi River, and then he pulled to a stop to watch the sun go down.

A Mississippi Sunset

"The sunsets here are gorgeous," said William as he slipped his arm around her waist. "The way it reflects off the river is really something. My sister once asked me to describe it to her but it was impossible."

As the sunset reflected off the wispy clouds, growing in intensity and turning a brilliant orange-red, Laura knew exactly how he felt. It would be difficult to describe.

Turning to him, she said, "If I were to describe this sunset... if it were possible..."

"Go on," he encouraged.

"It's not about the color. It's about the emotions it evokes inside you. Can you describe how this sunset makes you feel? You know... deep down inside?" Laura looked up into his eyes and smiled. "Do you understand what I mean?"

"I think I do," said William. "It's not about the color but the feelings it creates inside of me when I look at it. The joy. The happiness. The wonder of it."

Laura nodded. "Exactly. So tell me. How would you describe a Mississippi sunset now?"

Taking her hand, he gave it a gentle squeeze as he gazed at the exquisite colors before him. "It's absolutely lovely and brings joy to my soul. It's hard to explain the feelings I feel deep down inside. I'm happy. I'm content. And life couldn't be better." He turned to her and smiled. "Actually, it describes how I feel when I'm around you."

Laura was speechless. She didn't know what to say. His words touched her heart. To be compared to the sunset on the Mississippi was the greatest compliment he could have given her.

After the sunset faded away, he took her to an outdoor stage not far from the Mississippi. Lanterns were lit and an audience was gathered around the stage, listening to a group of singers that were accompanied by a banjo and guitar. The music was upbeat and cheerful.

When they concluded the song, one of the men stepped forward and announced, "Michael William Balfe wrote a romantic Irish operetta called: The Bohemian Girl. It was first performed in London in November of 1843... just last year. Our Miss Jennifer would now like to sing it for you: *I Dreamt I Dwelt in Marble Halls.*"

All was silent as a young dark-haired woman stepped forward. Giving a nod to the guitarist, he played an introduction. Clasping her hands together, the young lady looked down at her audience and began singing the aria.

Her voice was beautiful and the melody was delightful. When she sang the second verse, the message of the song touched Laura's heart like none other. It must have touched William as well, because he wrapped his arm around her and pulled her close.

I dreamt that suitors sought my hand,
That knights upon bended knee
And with vows no maiden's heart could

withstand,
They pledged their faith to me.
And I dreamt that one of that noble host
Came forth my hand to claim.
But I also dreamt, which charmed me most,
That you loved me still the same
That you loved me
You loved me still the same,
That you loved me
You loved me still the same.

Laura's heart melted and she knew what it was telling her. William was good for her. He was everything she had been searching for. The only problem now was how to tell her parents. How would they respond? They were convinced that Albert was the perfect match for her.

After the performance, William helped her into the buggy and took her home. The ride was peaceful and the moon above shined brightly.

Turning to her, William said softly, "I enjoyed our time together."

"Me, too."

Glancing down at her, he slipped his hand around hers and gave a gentle squeeze.

Gazing at their hands clasped together, Laura smiled. He was so affectionate and she liked that about him.

As he pulled his horse to a stop in front of her home, William asked, "Are you free tomorrow afternoon?"

She nodded.

"How about if I take you fishing?"

"Fishing?" she said with stunned surprise. "Are you serious?"

When he nodded, she broke into laughter. Horseraces and fishing? William was not the average suitor. That was for sure.

"Why not!" she said with humor. "That's something I have never done before."

"Good!"

With a grin, he hopped down from the buggy. Taking her hand, he helped her down and they walked to the porch.

Leaning his back against the railing, he asked, "What did you enjoy most tonight?"

She shrugged her shoulders. "All of it. But I do have to agree that the Mississippi sunsets are very beautiful. I was very impressed."

"I loved the musical entertainment," said William as he looked up at the stars above.

When he began humming the chorus from Marble Halls, Laura raised her brow and said, "You have a nice voice, William."

He turned to her and took her hand, pulling her towards him. "Why, thank you, Miss McBride. My father always sang hymns around the yard as he did his chores. In Pembrokeshire, he was the chorister for the church choir. And I belonged to it. Did you know the Welsh are known for their musical abilities?"

"Is that so?" she said in a teasing manner as she gazed up into his handsome face. "I'm sure you have no prejudice."

"Not at all. It's a fact," he replied softly as he looked into her eyes, giving her a message that caused her heart to skip a beat.

When she gently touched his cheek and gazed up into his eyes, Laura sensed the shift in his mood.

Enfolding her in his arms, he pressed his lips to hers. As she wrapped her arms around his neck, he deepened the kiss, causing her to melt into his arms. Being in his embrace felt so natural. She had only known him for a short while but it didn't take much to realize that she was undeniably in love. As he entangled his fingers in her hair, he gave her several warm kisses that weakened her knees.

When she sighed, he finally pulled back. Taking her by the shoulders, he said softly, "I'd better go before the preacher comes outside and tells me off." He gave her another kiss on the lips and smiled. "Sleep well. I hope you have lovely dreams tonight. I know I will. You're going to be right in the middle of them."

As he turned to leave, Laura asked, "What time tomorrow?"

He stopped in midstride and turned around. "Tomorrow?"

Laura was amused. It looked like her kisses had affected him good.

He cleared his throat and chuckled. "Oh yes! That's right. I'll pick you up around six. Is that fine with you?"

She nodded. "Thank you for a lovely evening, William. See you tomorrow."

As she watched him leave, Laura leaned against the railing. Her heart was beating like it never had before. She had fallen in love with a charming Welshman.

Then it dawned on her that her trials were just beginning. She knew her father would not approve. He had told her that he was giving her an education so she would marry well. They had already picked out a suitor for her. Besides that, it was personal. Albert's parents were dear friends of theirs. They both had agreed on the union and shook hands on it.

Laura knew that her parents wouldn't accept William. He did not have the qualities her father wanted. He was only a deputy sheriff. Being an immigrant was against him, as well.

Laura was in love with someone her parents would not approve of. What was she to do?

Chapter 11

As the end of the week drew near, William realized that Nicholas was going to put him on duty during the upcoming revival meetings. It would last three days, from Friday to Sunday, and he dreaded his assignment. While the two preachers expounded their doctrines, which differed quite a bit, William was supposed to mill around and find Frank.

Knowing he would not be able to spend much time with Laura, he wanted to make the most of his time with her.

Standing on the front porch, William pulled her into his arms and said, "Miss Laura McBride, I've lost my heart and I think you know who has stolen it from me. As you well know, I can't get along without it. Especially if I'm going to survive the next few days, listening to those revivalists preach."

Laura laughed as she snuggled into his arms. "Are you sure I have it?"

"Most definitely. The day you asked me to dance the Boston Waltz, I realized there was no one for me but you."

Pulling back, she said teasingly, "Don't let Preacher Armstrong hear that. You know how he feels about the waltz. It's wanton behavior."

He frowned and shook his head. "Please don't remind me."

Tilting her head curiously, she asked, "Do I really have your heart?"

"Of course. There's no doubt about it."

Laura bit her lip. With urgency, she said, "Promise me that you'll be careful. Don't take any chances, William. Please?"

Taking her hand, he pressed his lips to it. "I'll be careful. I promise." Gazing into her eyes, he asked, "Are you ready?"

"As ready as I'll ever be," she said excitedly. "You have taken me places that no suitor has ever taken me. I'm excited to see where you'll take me next."

He grinned. "I try to make it memorable."

"Oh yes. When you took me fishing and made me put a worm on my hook, that was very memorable."

"I was going to do it for you," he defended. "But you insisted that I teach you how to do it yourself."

Laura broke into laughter. "I know. I didn't know what I was getting myself into when I said it."

He chuckled. "And how about the fish that got away? That was memorable. Right?"

"Oh yes. Definitely. When I was trying to put it in the bucket, it slipped out of my hands and jumped into my lap. That was quite memorable, indeed. I was so shocked that I stood up, and it landed back in the water."

"They do get a bit wiggly, don't they," he said with laughter. "Just wait and see what I have planned for you today."

Taking her hand, he helped her into the buggy. Then climbing into his seat, he jiggled the reins and his horse took off down the road.

* * *

Laura was excited. William had surprised her with something new and different each time he took her some place. He was rather unconventional when it came to courting. How she wished she could tell her parents about her fishing excursion, but they wouldn't understand.

When they finally arrived at the Willow Valley City Park at the edge of the Mississippi River, Laura noticed several people milling around. One man was putting a rock slab in four different places evenly apart. Sam had a ball and was tossing it back and forth to a friend.

As William helped her down from the buggy, Sam hurried over to them and said, "Everyone's here. We set up some benches for the spectators." He chuckled. "Which are usually our families."

Nicholas walked up to Laura and said, "Glad you're here. If you want, you can sit by my wife."

He pointed to Felicity who was sitting with her three children. She recognized Hannah from the Hot Chocolate Shoppe and Angelica. But there were many others that she didn't recognize.

When William's sister saw them, Serenity hurried over to her and took her hand. "Come with me. You can sit with us."

Her Welsh accent was like music to her ears as she spoke. As they sat down on a bench, the women greeted her.

"I'm glad you could make it," said Felicity.

"Why are we here?" asked Laura. "William hasn't told me a thing."

Serenity laughed. "I guess he wanted to surprise you. He's such a rascal."

It was true. He kept surprising her each time he took her out.

Pointing to the men, Serenity said, "Have you heard of *Town Ball*?"

Laura shook her head.

"Some players call it *Round Ball* or *Rounders*."

"I'm not familiar with it," said Laura as she watched the men gather together.

Felicity leaned toward her and said, "We just call it *Base Ball*."

Pointing to the slabs of rock, Serenity explained, "Those are the bases. Some people have five but we've decided to only have four. The batter stands at the home plate and has three chances to hit the ball. If he doesn't hit it after three tries, he's out. If the batter hits the ball and it's caught after the first bounce, then he's out. If one person gets out, then they have to change places with the other team."

"They only get one chance and they're out?" said Laura with surprise.

"That's right."

"I think they should have three outs rather than just one."

Serenity shrugged. "Maybe they'll change the rules some day."

"Oh! We did change one rule," said Felicity as she glanced at her children. "If the other team throws a ball and hits the person who is running to a base, he's out. We changed that because we, as mothers, felt it was much too dangerous for our children. So we changed that rule. They have to touch them with the ball, instead."

Laura nodded, understanding her concern. It was a very intriguing game.

When William turned around and noticed that she was watching him, he winked, letting her know that he was glad she had come.

Felicity nudged her and said, "Nicholas told me that William is quite smitten with you."

She turned to her and smiled. "I feel the same way about him."

Felicity clapped her hands together. "I knew it. I just knew it. You will never find a better fellow in all of Willow Valley. He is so kind and generous. William always thinks of others before himself and definitely supports your cause. Fighting for the rights of others is important to him."

Laura's heart melted at her words and a tear trickled down her cheek.

Placing a hand on hers, Serenity said with concern, "What's wrong? Are you all right?"

"Everything Felicity said is true," she said as she wiped the tear from her face. "I could never find a better man than William. He's supportive and so affectionate. I've fallen in love with him without a doubt."

She bit her lip as more tears welled up in her eyes.

"He feels the same way about you. He told me so." Tilting her head curiously, Serenity said, "I don't understand. Why the tears?"

"Was it something I said?" asked Felicity with concern.

Laura shook her head. "No, no. It's nothing you said. It's my parents. I know they won't approve. They sent me to Troy Seminary to get an education so I would marry well. You know what I mean."

Serenity and Felicity both nodded.

"While I was going to school, my parents picked out a husband for me... someone from our previous home. Our parents are good friends and he has agreed to court me. They say he is a perfect match and asked me to give him a chance. Out of respect for my parents, I agreed."

"An arranged marriage?" asked Felicity with stunned surprise.

"It's more common than you think," said Serenity.

"When they meet William, I'm sure they'll understand why you love him," said Felicity with confidence.

A Mississippi Sunset

Laura gave a deep sigh. Felicity did not understand. Albert was the son of a very good friend. It was personal.

Taking her skirt, Laura wiped the tears from her face. "Don't worry about me. I'll figure something out."

"Play ball!" yelled Nicholas.

With that announcement, the spectators turned to the men and watched them play a game that was quite entertaining. Every time someone got out, the teams would trade places. According to Felicity, the pitcher could only throw the ball underhanded.

When Sam hit the ball, it went flying through the air and everyone cheered. But it didn't last long. William caught the ball after one bounce. Sam was out and everyone had to change places once again.

Finally it was William's turn at bat. As he walked up to the home plate with the bat in hand, he smiled at Laura and winked. He was so adorable whenever he flirted with her. She couldn't have found a more amiable and affectionate man in her life.

When the pitcher threw the ball, William hit it with a smack and it went flying through the air and over the heads of all the men.

"I got it! I got it!" yelled Sam as he backed up, hoping to catch the ball.

Fortunately, it went over his head, just barely, and flew into the Mississippi River. A cheer filled the air as William ran to first base, second base, third base, and finally to home plate.

Nicholas furrowed his brow. "That was a great hit, Will. But did you have to sink it into the Mississippi?"

All out of breath, William laughed. "Sorry. I'll buy another ball before the next game."

Nicholas chuckled as he patted his back. "You do that!"

"Games over!" announced Sam. "William's team won! But it won't happen again if I have anything to do with it."

Angelica and Hannah waved to Laura as they walked toward her.

"This game is new to me," said Hannah. "I'm originally from England and the closest thing to this is Cricket."

After conversing for a while, everyone bid farewell and William took Laura home. It was dusk when they finally stepped on the porch of her home.

"I had a wonderful time," said William. "I hope you did, too."

She nodded. "I enjoyed it very much. When you have someone to cheer for, that always makes it more fun."

Leaning his back against the railing, William motioned for her to come to him.

When she glanced at her neighbor's home, she saw Preacher Armstrong peeking out the window. With a shake of her head, she said, "Don't tempt me, William. The preacher is watching us."

A Mississippi Sunset

William glanced over his shoulder and he grinned. "He's probably bored stiff and needs a little entertainment in his life."

Laura broke into laughter and shook her head. "You can't be serious. He's a very sober fellow and very strict."

"Shall we go inside?"

"No!" She shook her head adamantly. "That would definitely give him something to talk about. You need to behave, William. I don't want the preacher to spread rumors about me."

He sobered. "Oh no. I wouldn't want that. You mean too much to me." With a tender smile, he stepped toward her and took her hand. "You can at least stand beside me. There's no harm in that."

Laura gave him a coy smile. As he held her hand, William caressed her palm as they talked about the ballgame and his upcoming assignment at the revival.

"I hope you find the man who broke into my home," said Laura.

"Me, too."

Kissing her cheek, he said, "I'd better go. I'm going to have a big day tomorrow and the next and the next." Bringing her hand to his lips, he gave it a lingering kiss. "I'll see you after the revival meetings are over."

As he walked toward his buggy, Laura sighed. He was the most romantic man she had ever gotten to know. How she wished she could explain to her parents that she didn't want to marry Albert and was in love with someone else!

There just had to be a way. There had to be a solution to her problem. But what was it?

Chapter 12

All day William listened to speeches full of repentance, hell-fire and damnation. Once in a while the preacher would burst into song and soon his followers would join in. While he was searching for Frank, the sheriff asked the militia to look around for Copeland's Gang. They couldn't wear their uniforms or it would warn the gang of their presence. They had to appear just like anyone else in the audience, searching for the truth.

Although, William didn't feel Preacher McGrath had that much truth to offer. And Preacher Armstrong didn't impress him, either. He seemed a bit too self-righteous.

As William nonchalantly scanned the area for Frank, he tried his best not to stand out or be noticed. As the sun was about to go down, he finally saw the man he was searching for. He was at the back of the congregation. Quickly, William made his way toward the end of the field, but Frank noticed him and snuck into the forest.

Following the miscreant, William entered the woods and began searching. The man had disappeared and was nowhere in sight. William groaned, realizing he had lost him once again. When he heard the crunching of leaves behind him, he was about to turn around when he felt strong arms wrap around his neck and chest.

"Are you following me?" asked a gruff voice, as he held tight to William.

The man was strong and shorter than William, but he had a firm hold on him, and he couldn't break loose.

"What makes you think I'm following you?"

"No use denying it, Deputy. I know who you are. You're not very good at tracking people, are you?"

Since the man knew who he was, William decided to use some diplomacy. "I'm looking for a man by the name of Frank McLaughlin. Are you that man?"

"Who wants to know?"

"The sheriff wants to ask you some questions. All I have to do is bring you in. After you answer his questions to his satisfaction, you are free to leave. It's as simple as that."

"Nothing is that simple," growled Frank as he squeezed his arms tightly around William. "What does he want?"

"I'm not here to do you any harm, Frank. Let me go so I can explain."

"You've got sixty seconds to explain," said Frank in a threatening tone. "Or you're a dead man."

Realizing his dire situation, William asked him one pertinent question. "Did you break into a young woman's home two weeks ago for the intent of robbing her?"

Frank chuckled. "Is that why you're here?"

"Yes. Did you?"

"I didn't steal nothin' if that's what you're askin'. She was a feisty one. I didn't expect her to be a she-cat. She went after me like a banshee with a broom in her hand."

William chuckled. "Are you serious? You poor man!"

Sensing that Frank was distracted, William quickly took advantage of the situation and jabbed his elbow into the man's chest. When he grunted and loosened his grip, William broke loose and quickly turned around. With an uppercut, he swung his fist into the man's chin. His head whipped backwards and Frank crumpled to the ground. William had learned one thing about fighting. An uppercut to the chin usually put a man out instantly. It was the quickest way to end a fight.

Hefting the man over his shoulder, he carried him to his horse and laid him over the saddle. Taking the reins, William guided his horse into town and toward the sheriff's office.

When Nicholas saw him arrive, he walked outside to greet him. "What do we have here?"

After tying the reins to a hitching post, William pulled the unconscious man off his horse and carried him over his shoulder into the sheriff's office.

As Nicholas followed him inside, he asked with surprise, "Is that who I think it is? Why is he unconscious?"

After Nicholas opened the jail cell, William plopped the man down on a bed and allowed the sheriff to lock the door.

"You asked why he's unconscious? Well, he wouldn't come along willingly. There wasn't anything I could do."

Nicholas chuckled as he stared at their prisoner. "Good job, Deputy. Now get that pretty young lady of yours, and let's have her identify him."

William smiled when he heard Laura being referred to as *his* young lady. He most certainly felt that way. As he was about to leave, the door burst open and a few militiamen pushed a half dozen rough-looking men into the room.

Holding a pistol in his hand, Jonathan said, "We caught them stealing some horses. I believe they belong to that gang you were telling us about. The Wages and Copeland Gang." He gave a shove to the man in front of him. "Get moving! You hear me?"

William smiled when he noticed how tough Jonathan sounded.

"This way," said William as he motioned to two other jail cells. "As you can see, we already have someone in this one."

Jonathan escorted the prisoners into their new living quarters. No one said a word. As the men obediently walked into the jail cell, it was easy to see they were not happy about their

A Mississippi Sunset

situation. Hearing the commotion, Frank groaned and slowly sat up in bed. When he saw the new prisoners, he frowned.

"According to Sheriff Carter, the leaders of the Wages and Copeland Gang have been too elusive to catch," said Nicholas. "But we have figured out their secret. They like revivals. It won't be long until we catch up to Copeland and Wages."

"If you think you're going to catch them, you're dreaming," said Frank as he rubbed his sore jaw. Getting to his feet, he sauntered toward the bars and furrowed his brow. "They're always in disguise. They've never been caught and never will be. Each disguise is ingenious."

Turning to Nicholas, William said, "It sounds like Frank knows something we don't. What do you think?"

"I believe you're right."

"I'll be back," said William. "I have to get my witness."

With that said, he headed out the door and rode toward Laura's home. As he rapped at her door, no one answered so he walked around the house and found Laura kneeling in the dirt, weeding and talking to her flowers, as usual. He grinned at the sight.

As he walked toward her, she turned and looked up at him. With a cheerful smile, Laura said, "William! It's so nice to see you." Dusting off her hands, she motioned for him to take a seat beside her. "Are you off duty all ready?"

He shook his head. "Not quite. I have one more thing to do before I can go home."

"And what's that?" she asked in her usual coy manner that almost drove him crazy.

Kneeling down beside her, he cupped her face in his hands and pressed his lips to hers. Since Armstrong's house was not in view, he felt he could get away with it.

When she gave a tender sigh, William smiled and said, "Would you like to identify the intruder who broke into your home?"

Laura nodded. "Did you find him?"

"I sure did."

"How?"

"He was at the revival meeting and I sort of stumbled into him. When I asked him about you, he called you a feisty she-cat." He chuckled. "That's a side of you that I haven't seen, yet."

Laura bit her lip and shrugged. "He made me mad."

Taking her hand, he helped her to her feet. "I need you to come with me down to the sheriff's office."

"Let me wash up first and change into something fresh," she said as she dusted the dirt off her hands.

With that said, she hurried toward the back door. While she was getting ready, William got her horse and buggy hitched up and ready to go. When she returned, he helped her into her seat.

"Since your assignment is done, I bet you're going to miss all those revival meetings," Laura said teasingly.

"Balderdash!" said William as he climbed into the buggy and took the reins.

She laughed. "It sounds like you didn't put your whole heart into this assignment. Didn't you feel the spirit coming over you? Didn't you join in and sing those hymns with your lovely Welsh voice? That should have got you in the spirit."

Seeing the teasing glint in her eyes, he took her hand and kissed it. "You adorable young lady! The only thing that the spirit is telling me now is... is..." He touched her face and gazed into her lovely eyes, wondering how she felt about him. When she leaned toward him and gave him a warm kiss, he was not able to help himself. So he blurted out, "Marry me, Laura. Please marry me."

As her eyes widened, she said, "What did you say?"

"I know we've only known each other for a short time, but I'm in love with you. You're the only one for me. I know that without a doubt." Cocking his head, he asked, "Do you love me?"

Laura gave him the usual coy smile. "Perhaps."

"Don't tease me. I'm serious."

Nodding, she said softly, "Oh William, I do. With all my heart. And I think you know that by now."

With a breath of relief, he asked, "When are your parents coming back home so I can ask your father for your hand in marriage?"

"Tomorrow afternoon." She bit her lip and shook her head. "But we have one problem. He won't give you permission."

Furrowing his brow, he said, "I don't understand."

"My parents have already picked out a suitor for me. They are determined to have Albert as their new son-in-law. He's someone from back home. Our fathers have been good friends for years. I'm sure they had this planned years in advance. It's all been arranged."

"Are you engaged to him?"

"No. Not yet."

William smiled. "In that case, can't you just tell your father that you're in love with someone else?"

Laura shook her head. "His mind is made up. If you ask for my hand and he refuses you… and if we go against his wishes and get married anyway… he won't accept you because we ignored his wishes. I'm not sure what we can do."

"How about your mother? Does she feel the same way?"

Laura gave a sigh. "I'm afraid so."

William thought for a moment, trying to figure out a solution. When a brilliant idea formed in his mind, his eyes brightened with hope. It was perfect. Whether it was divine inspiration or not, he thought it would work.

Giving a sly grin, he said, "I have an idea."

"You do?"

He kissed her sweet lips and said, "How about if we let them get to know me first? I can show them what I'm made of."

With laughter, she asked teasingly, "Will you sing to them?"

He chuckled. Then he went into detail what they could do, but it would involve getting help from their dear friends.

As he explained his brilliant plan to her, he said, "What do you think?"

Laura bit her lip and thought for a moment. With a nod, she said, "I don't know if it will work, but I'm all for it." She snuggled into his arms and kissed his cheek. "Let's do it. We don't have much time to get everything arranged, though."

"I know. So we'll have to work fast." After giving the reins a snap, the horse took off down the road. "Now let's identify Frank."

When they arrived at the sheriff's office, William guided her to the jail cell.

Stepping up to the bars, she examined the prisoner. "Yes, that's the man," said Laura with a shudder. "I will never forget that face."

As Frank rose from his bed, he furrowed his brow. He didn't look happy to see her.

"You she-cat!" he yelled as he lunged for the bars.

Quickly William pulled her away just as the prisoner stuck his arms through, trying to grab her. He looked as if he was reliving the day she had pummeled him with the broom.

"You'll regret the day you met me," he growled. "You beat me good and you won't get away with it."

"She beat you?" asked one of the prisoners in the next cell.

"She battered me over the head with a broom and chased me down the street."

"That little lady actually hit you with a broom and you ran away?" asked another prisoner with disbelief. "Are you that spineless?"

Nicholas chuckled when he heard the prisoner's rebuke. "If Frank McLaughlin hadn't broken into Laura's home, I wouldn't have found out that he belonged to the Copeland gang. That was when I realized that the rest of you were probably milling around, as well. In other words, he's the very reason you men were caught. How about that!"

"What did you do, Frank?" growled one of the prisoners. "You drew attention to us because of your lustful ways. I can't believe it. We wouldn't have been caught if not for you. When Copeland finds out, you had better watch out."

"I saw her preachin' at the Town Square. Since I've been workin' so hard, McGrath told me I could have the day off, so I decided to have some fun and…"

"Shut up! Just shut up, Frank," yelled one of the prisoners."

With great curiosity, Nicholas walked up to the cell and asked, "Why did Preacher McGrath say you could have the day off? Do you work for him?"

A Mississippi Sunset

"We don't know the man," growled the other prisoner. "You hear me? There was a revival meetin' and we decided to attend."

Giving a knowing smile, Nicholas turned to William and said, "Bring in McGrath. I'd like to have a talk with him."

With a nod, he said, "I have to take Laura home, first. Is that all right?"

Nicholas nodded. "If I'm right, Preacher McGrath is not really a preacher, after all. I suspect he may be one of the gang. That's a pretty good disguise, if you ask me."

"Don't listen to Frank," growled one of the prisoners. "He don't know nothin'. He's just a lousy horse thief."

All six prisoners looked quite upset at Frank. They stared at him with daggers in their eyes.

After William took Laura home, he and Sam arrived at the field where the preacher had set up his tent. McGrath and the tent were nowhere to be found. He usually stayed for three days to do his preaching, but he disappeared after one day. Was he really part of the gang? If so, that was a perfect disguise. As he preached repentance, the gang robbed the people.

After William reported what he found, Nicholas sat down at his desk and shook his head. "Disappearing after one day of preaching makes him look guilty. What do you think?"

"That was my conclusion, as well."

"I'm going to send word to Sheriff Carter what we just discovered." When William chuckled, Nicholas asked, "What's so funny?"

"How many folks were listening to an outlaw preach and believed every word he said? As he told them to repent of their sins, he was stealing from them. But that's not all. How many people were baptized by a criminal? How many marriages were performed? Are they even legal? And if not, then what?"

Nicholas crossed his arms over his chest and smiled. "Talking about marriages, do I see a certain look in your eyes whenever you're around Laura? Are you considering the idea of settling down?"

William nodded as he took a seat across from Nicholas. "I proposed to her tonight and she accepted. I think I might find another job. It's too dangerous being a lawman. If I wouldn't have elbowed Frank like I did, I don't think he would have been merciful to me. In his business, he can't have witnesses."

Nicholas sighed. "Sam is only part time because he's going to college, and I'm losing you to a woman. Both are very noble causes. What can I say? When you find another job, let me know and I'll start looking for someone to take your place."

William got to his feet and nodded. "I've got to go. Laura and I have to prepare for her parents' arrival."

After telling Nicholas about their plans, the sheriff broke into laughter. "I sure hope it works. Good luck!"

"I don't need luck. I need a miracle. That's what I need."

Nicholas gave a curt nod. "In my opinion, that's exactly what you'll need."

William chuckled and headed out the door. As he climbed onto his horse, he thought about Laura. She was everything he desired in a woman. Without a doubt, he was deeply and undeniably in love with her.

When he had explained his idea to her, it sounded good to him. In his experiences, though, something always happened that would prevent his little scheme from working. But what could possibly happen to disrupt or ruin their plans?

Linda Weaver Clarke

Chapter 13

Laura was excited to see her parents. When they pulled up to the house, she did not expect to see a certain gentleman sitting beside them. When Albert agreed to court her, she didn't expect him to show up at Willow Valley with her parents. What was she to do?

She needed time to convince her parents that William was the man for her. Since Albert was present, it would be difficult. She had to be careful what she said in front of him or their plan would be ruined.

As they climbed down from the family buggy, her mother said, "Guess who we brought back with us?"

Laura nodded. "Welcome to our humble home, Albert. It's been a few years, hasn't it?"

He stared at their home with a critical eye and then turned to her. With a smile, he said in a Southern accent, "Yes it has. The last time I saw you was when your parents sent you to that ladies school in New York." His eyes scanned her figure. "You have changed. Very fashionable, indeed!"

She cleared her throat and ignored his compliment. "Would you like to get freshened up?"

"That sounds wonderful," said Albert. "I'm sure Mabel and Arthur would like to freshen up, as well."

Her mother nodded. "Oh yes. I feel a bit dusty. We stopped off at a town not far from here to stay the night."

Albert shook his head and groaned. "We stayed at a dreadful hotel. I'll never go there again."

"Oh, it wasn't so bad," said Mabel. "They were helpful and made sure we were comfortable."

Albert shook his head and whispered to Laura, "She's always so kind to the lower class. Personally, I didn't think their service was that good."

Leading Albert into the house, Laura showed him the guest room. While everyone was freshening up, she decided to do as William had suggested... introduce her parents to a few residents of Willow Valley and then to William. She wanted them to get to know him impartially before giving them the news.

They knew Laura's independent nature. When she believed in a cause, there was no stopping her. But telling them about her love for William was different and it would not be easy. The timing had to be just right.

After everyone gathered together in the front room, Laura asked her parents if she could show them around Willow Valley and introduce them to her friends. They were up for it, which delighted her.

As her father climbed into the back seat of the family buggy, he said, "Your mother and I can sit back here while Albert sits up front with you."

"That's a great idea, Arthur," exclaimed her mother.

He grinned. "I thought so."

Laura groaned inwardly, hoping her mother would sit with her. But her parents had different ideas.

The first place she took them was to have the most delicious drink she had ever tasted. She led them into Hannah's Hot Chocolate Shoppe and ordered four cups of hot chocolate.

As Hannah filled the order, she said, "Wasn't that baseball game the best ever? The scores were real close. It wasn't until William hit the ball into the Mississippi that we won that one. Thomas was quite elated since he was on the winning team."

"Oh yes. It was so entertaining," said Laura. "I loved it."

Albert furrowed his brow. "You went to a baseball game?" He shook his head. "I went to one but didn't see what all the fuss was about. It was quite boring, watching someone throw a ball and bat it into the air." He groaned. "It's a very tedious sport, if you ask me."

Laura hoped he wouldn't be this negative when meeting the rest of her friends.

As Hannah handed a cup of chocolate to each of her customers, Laura introduced her parents and Albert to her.

"This is Hannah," she told her parents with great pride. "She actually owns this shop and it's doing quite well."

Laura could tell that it took her father and Albert by surprise.

With a raise of her brow, Mabel exclaimed, "Is that so? I'm impressed."

With a gentle smile, Hannah said, "Your daughter is a real asset to this community. She is awakening the residence to the truth and making a difference here."

Mabel smiled. "That's nice to hear. She told me a little about her adventures in her letters but not much. I'm sure we'll hear all about it tonight at supper." Staring at her curiously, she said, "You're from England, aren't you?"

Hannah laughed. "Did my accent give me away?"

"It sure did. Have you been here long?"

"No, not long. About five years."

"I can't imagine how difficult it would be, pulling up roots and beginning life afresh in a strange new world." Taking a sip of her chocolate, Mabel said, "This is very delicious. It looks like you're succeeding to me. Who could resist such a delightful drink?"

"Thank you, Mrs. McBride."

After finishing their hot chocolate, they headed to the Willow Valley News so she could introduce them to Angelica.

As they walked up to her desk, she said, "Mother... Father, I'd like to introduce my dear friend to you, Angelica Morgan. Her husband owns this paper. She writes articles for the Willow Valley News, usually controversial ones of a political nature. Her articles are very impressive."

Albert frowned. "Controversial articles of a political nature? I'm sure they must be one sided, being a woman and all. I've never met a female who knows that much about politics."

Clearing his throat, Simon Morgan walked up to them and said firmly, "I beg to differ with you, sir. It is my wife's articles that help me sell my paper. And they are never one-sided. She investigates, reports, and then gives her opinion."

Albert nodded and said in a gentlemanly manner, "Pardon me, sir. I didn't mean to offend."

Ignoring what Albert said, Angelica turned to Laura's parents and said, "You would be proud of your daughter. She gave a lecture at the cathedral for the youth and encouraged them to get an education and to develop their talents. She also told them to fight for the right to vote. All we need is one state to make a change and the rest would eventually follow."

Albert shook his head. "It'll never happen. Trust me." Turning to Laura, he said, "I'm surprised that you would get their hopes up like that. You shouldn't say such things, Laura."

When Angelica got to her feet, ready to defend her, Laura quickly shook her head. She knew what her friend was about to say and didn't want a scene in front of her parents.

"Besides that," Albert continued. "Speaking in public and giving lectures isn't lady like. My pastor says that it threatens the female character and can cause permanent mental injury."

"Nonsense!" exclaimed Angelica.

"Balderdash!" exclaimed Simon. "I don't believe it."

Not wanting a scene, she quickly took her mother's arm and said, "I'd like to show you Town Square. It's beautiful."

Leading her outside, she saw Felicity, teaching an art class at the park. With a smile, Laura waved to her and Felicity motioned her over.

As they approached, Laura said, "Mother, this is Felicity, a very good friend of mine. She taught art at the Troy Seminary in New York."

Mabel's eyes brightened. "You did? What a pleasure it is to meet you! Why did you leave such a prestigious school?"

As they shook hands, Felicity said, "My father passed on so I came home to be with my mother."

"Oh, I'm so sorry," said Mabel. "My condolences."

Motioning to the art students who were painting, Laura said, "She's doing some good here in Willow Valley, as you can see. She has students of all ages and they love her because of her kind nature."

Albert stared at Felicity with great curiosity and said, "Very interesting, indeed. Most schoolteachers don't look like you. They pull their hair into a tight bun and don't usually wear fashionable clothes. Their attitude is firm and strict and unrelenting."

It was true. She was a beautiful woman.

With a tender smile, Felicity said, "I'm so glad you sent your daughter to Troy Seminary. It's an excellent school. Laura has taken what she learned there and is helping others."

Arthur smiled at his daughter. "We're proud of her accomplishments."

"She gave a lecture right here in Town Square not long ago." Pointing to the gazebo, Felicity said, "Laura stood over there and talked about freedom."

"A good subject, to be sure," agreed Arthur.

"She explained how wrong it is to have a man in bondage. It is against the laws of God and any Christian should know that. She gave a powerful speech, sir, and you would have been proud of her."

"I can't believe it," blurted out Albert. "The plantation owners would loose their crops if not for their servants."

"Then they should pay their workers just like any other businessman," Felicity said firmly. "If we do as Laura suggested, to not buy any products from the South, they will know we mean business."

Albert turned to Laura with widened eyes. "You actually encouraged such a thing?"

She nodded but did not say a word. Felicity was doing a good enough job defending her.

Turning to Felicity, he said, "That's why women like you shouldn't get into politics. What does a woman know about business, anyway?"

"She's not just any woman," said a firm voice behind them. "She's my wife."

With a gentle smile, Felicity said, "This is my husband, Sheriff Nicholas Adamson."

Albert's eyes widened when he saw the tall muscular lawman standing behind him. "Pardon me, sir. I shouldn't have said that." Turning to Laura he said firmly, "When we're married, you will not be giving any more lectures on this subject. You are lucky that someone didn't try to tar and feather you."

"What did you say?" said Felicity with surprise. "Marry you? I'm sorry but..."

Quickly, Laura shook her head and placed a finger to her lips. Felicity glanced at her husband and he gave a slight nod. She got the message.

Nicholas turned to Albert. "Just to let you know, a few men didn't take kindly to what she said. But my deputy took care of them and booted them out. She is a good influence in Willow Valley and we're glad to have her."

"You see!" exclaimed Albert. "You were lucky the law was around."

Laura gave a gentle smile as she remembered that day. "Oh yes. But not lucky. Very blessed."

A Mississippi Sunset

William's plan was working. He said that it would open her parents' eyes. They would see what kind of woman she really was through the eyes of her friends. But it was doing more than that. It was opening their eyes to what kind of person Albert was.

The next place she took them was to visit Mary, her dearest friend. She had relatives who didn't see anything wrong with involuntary servitude, but she was adamantly against it. Hopefully the subject wouldn't come up again because she didn't like Albert's belligerent attitude.

When they pulled up to the house, Laura was pleasantly surprised to see Serenity sitting on the porch and visiting with Mary.

As Laura approached, Mary jumped from her seat and hurried to Laura. Wrapping her arms around her, she said, "You brought your parents by to meet me, didn't you?" Stepping back, she extended her hand to Mabel. "I'm Laura's friend, Mary. It's so nice to meet you."

"Like wise," said Mabel as they shook hands.

"Your daughter is such a sweetheart. She's really making a difference here."

Arthur chuckled. "That's what we hear." He patted Albert's back. "This gentleman at my side is Albert. His father is a dear friend of mine."

Motioning toward the porch, Mary said, "This is Serenity Davies."

"It's nice to meet you," said Serenity as she stepped down from the porch.

With great pride, Laura said, "She teaches a reading and writing class for adults right here in town."

"Do you have a degree?" asked Albert with a raise of his brow. "A teacher must have an education, you know."

"I graduated from a private boarding school in Wales," said Serenity. "When I arrived here, I noticed that many Americans couldn't write their name or even read. So I decided to help them. Trust me. I know what I'm doing, sir."

Her attitude, the way she spoke, and the way she reacted to Albert gave her the appearance of a refined and noble lady. Surprised at her demeanor, Albert seemed speechless.

Laura tried to think of another subject to talk about but her dear friend beat her to it.

"Wasn't the horse race exciting?" said Mary. "I've never heard a group cheer so loudly, as they did that day."

"Oh yes," said Laura with an eager nod. "It was so entertaining." Laura turned to Serenity and winked at her. "I rather enjoyed it."

"You went to a horse race?" asked Albert with stunned surprise. "I hope you women had a chaperone. There are a lot of undesirables at a horserace. I go regularly and quite enjoy it. When we're married, I'll take you to see a real horserace. You'll see a big difference from a small town one. Only professional riders are accepted."

A Mississippi Sunset

"Married?" gasped Serenity. She blinked a couple of times and stared at Laura questioningly. "Pardon me, sir, but..."

"Albert is the man I told you about at the ballgame," said Laura. "Remember?"

Mary quickly touched Serenity's arm and nodded, not wanting their secret to slip out.

Giving a nod, Serenity understood. "Oh, yes. I see."

After a short visit with her friends, Laura was thoroughly embarrassed by Albert's attitude. When he mentioned that women should know their place in society, both Mary and Serenity glared at the man.

As they rode away, she tried to ignore him but found it difficult. She jiggled the reins and the horse picked up speed.

Not able to hold back any longer, she said firmly, "I would appreciate it if you wouldn't insult my friends when your opinion differs with theirs."

Albert frowned. "What do you mean by that?"

She didn't say another word. Laura was too disgusted with his closed mind.

Glancing at her parents in the back seat, she said, "I'd like to introduce you to the deputy of Willow Valley. He's a good man. When I was hanging a bunch of fliers all over town, he helped me. He also introduced me to Hannah's Hot Chocolate. Serenity is his sister."

"Really?" said Mabel with great interest. "She's such a lovely lady. So refined."

"Remember the man who broke into our home that I wrote to you about?"

"Oh yes. I was so worried about you."

"Deputy Davies found him and arrested him. He was a known criminal who was stealing horses and whatnot."

"Is Davies the one who stopped those hecklers during your lecture?" Arthur asked curiously.

"Yes, the very one. He picked one up by his breeches and escorted him off the premises."

"Well… by all means," said Arthur with a firm nod. "I'd like to meet such a man."

Laura smiled when she heard her father's comment. He seemed genuinely interested in meeting William. Since Albert had been so negative after meeting each of her friends, she hoped that her parents would see that their matchmaking was a mistake.

When they drove up to the sheriff's office, William was sitting on the porch bench with a newspaper in his hand. When he looked up from his paper, a grin split across his face and his eyes lit up. His charming smile undid her, just like always. Laura was sure it was one of the reasons she had fallen in love with him.

He quickly got to his feet and headed to the buggy. Extending his hand out to Laura, she took it and a thrill went through her as he helped her down. Deep inside her soul, she prayed that God would help them convince her parents why William was a perfect match for her.

When she turned to her parents, Laura noticed that her mother was looking at William with great interest.

With a questioning look in her eyes, Mabel asked, "Is this Deputy Davies?"

Laura bit her lip and nodded. Had her mother seen the way William had looked at her and the way he had smiled?

After everyone climbed down from the buggy, Arthur said, "I understand you're the young man who found the known felon that broke into our home."

"Yes, sir. I did."

"And you stopped a ruckus when Laura was giving a lecture down at Town Square."

"Yes, sir. I did."

"And you introduced her to the most delicious hot chocolate I've ever tasted in my life."

William grinned. "Yes, sir. I certainly did."

Arthur held out his hand to William. "For those three things alone, I'm glad to meet you, young man. It looks like this town has good lawmen to keep the order."

"We try to make it safe for everyone, sir. But we do get riff-raff here every now and then."

"I met your sister. I found out that she teaches an evening class."

William smiled and gave a nod. "Yes, sir, she does. Serenity is a very talented lady. She has a lovely singing voice, too. Every day as she does her chores, she attracts the raccoons to our door with her singing. I'm sure you've heard how the

Welsh are musically talented. Well, she inherited that from her ancestors." He looked at Laura and grinned. "It's a known fact."

Laura broke into laughter and soon everyone joined in, except for Albert. He seemed a little suspicious of the way William was looking at her, whom he considered to be his future bride. Wrapping his arm around her waist, he pulled her close but she quickly pulled away from him.

Mabel gazed at her daughter curiously. Then turning to William, she asked, "Do you expect to be a deputy for the rest of your life?"

He shook his head and chuckled. "No, ma'am. At the moment, I'm looking for a better job. One that isn't so risky and dangerous. I understand that our former sheriff is related to you."

Arthur nodded. "He's my brother. He encouraged us to move out here and I'm glad we did. I know we're going to love it here."

Albert frowned as he stared at William. Narrowing his eyes, he gave William a message that made Laura uncomfortable.

Pulling her close to his side, Albert said, "When we get married, I'm not sure if we'll stay here. Depends."

"Not sure?" said Arthur with surprise. "But this is such a nice community and you can help me start my new business."

Albert shrugged his shoulders and didn't answer.

When Laura tried to tactfully get loose from his grasp, she was unable. She didn't want to

A Mississippi Sunset

make a scene so she decided to give up. It wasn't worth it.

When she saw William furrow his brow, Laura realized that he didn't like the way Albert was being so possessive. Hoping William would get the message, she shook her head. She didn't want him to cause a scene.

"Uhm... Mother, guess what? You'll be impressed to hear that William was a volunteer militiaman before he became a deputy. And he has a lovely voice, too. William sings quite well. You know the Welshmen. They are quite the singers."

"You're on a first name basis with this man?" complained Albert. Apparently, he had had enough, so he pulled her toward the buggy. "Let's go. I don't like the way he's ogling you."

"Ogling? He was doing no such thing. He's a gentleman and he treats me like a lady... unlike you."

"What do you mean by that? Unlike me?"

William stepped forward with clenched fists and said with authority, "Let go of my wife! Do you hear me?"

Arthur and Albert stared at William with shock and astonishment, but not Mabel. She was nodding. Apparently she had figured out that Laura was in love with him.

When Albert released his hold on her, she stepped toward William and he wrapped his arm around her in a protective manner. They had to elope. There was no other choice.

Shaking his head, Arthur asked with confusion, "Why didn't you tell us?"

Laura slid her hand into William's and gave a gentle squeeze. "You kept raving about me marrying well. You didn't want me to struggle as you and Mother did when you were first married. But Father... that is what life is all about. Struggles. Toiling together to make a better life. Would you have listened to me?"

Arthur shook his head and sighed. "When I saw how Albert reacted to everything you were doing and everything you believed in, I realized he wasn't meant for you. Each comment he made cut you deep... but you said nothing. Why?"

"I didn't want to make a scene."

With great concern, Mabel asked, "Do you think a marriage between a Welshman and an American will work? There's a lot of give and take in a marriage and you both come from different backgrounds. It may not be as easy as you think."

William looked down at Laura and smiled. "We'll be fine, Mrs. McBride. I love your daughter with all my heart. I promise you that I'll take care of her."

Albert threw his hands in the air with disgust. "How about me? I traveled all this way for nothing. And for a woman who doesn't even know her place in society. I wasted my time. A woman who speaks publicly is unwomanly, if you ask me."

A Mississippi Sunset

Without hesitation, William stepped forward, swung his fist back and gave it to him right in the face. Albert fell backwards against the buggy and quickly held his bleeding nose.

With narrowed eyes, William growled, "Don't... and I repeat, don't ever call my wife unwomanly. I'm getting sick and tired of hearing such rubbish. Get out of town this instant or I'll put you on a stage myself."

Albert furrowed his brow and said, "I'll sue you. I'll sue you for everything you've got."

William shrugged. "That's not much. Go ahead."

Helping Albert into the buggy, Arthur said, "Don't worry. I'll buy him a ticket on the first coach out of town. This is my fault."

"You do that!" said William as he rubbed his knuckles.

"Come over for supper after Albert's gone," said Mabel as she climbed into the buggy. "I'd like to find out what my new son-in-law is like."

As they pulled away, William turned to Laura and said, "Our plan didn't go as smoothly as I had hoped. But then... I didn't expect a suitor to show up and botch things. I wanted them to see how you have affected this community and what I was like before introducing your new husband to them."

She laughed. "It was best this way because my parents got to see what a snob Albert really is." Laura tilted her head curiously and said, "I'm surprised to see how my parents accepted you because they had their heart set on me marrying their friend's son. We didn't give them a chance to get to know you like we had planned."

He grinned as he raised his brow. "Eloping was the secret. We didn't go against their wishes. Am I right? We just didn't give them a choice. They had to accept me."

Laura placed her hand on his cheek and smiled. "Getting married last night was your idea... and an ingenious one it was."

"You think so?"

"Definitely." When Laura noticed that he was rubbing his knuckles, she took his hand and examined it. Tilting her head, she asked, "Did you get hurt?"

He grinned. "A kiss will make it better."

She brought his hand to her lips and gave his knuckles a gentle kiss. "I can soak them in Witch Hazel. That should help."

William smiled affectionately. "You and I, Laura... we're opposites. We're from two different backgrounds and we have differences of opinions, but that doesn't matter. Our goal is to make each other happy. That's what is important. Love knows no bounds when two people respect and support one another. If marriage is an equal partnership, then we can work together. Don't you think so?"

Laura nodded and said coyly, "Perhaps."

William laughed. "I'm serious. Give and take! That is what it is all about." Gazing into her eyes, he said, "I made a vow when I became your

A Mississippi Sunset

husband that I would support you in all your endeavors."

"Likewise," she said with affection. Laura touched his cheek. "One day someone will put together an organization supporting women's rights. Just wait and see!"

As she thought about it, Laura wondered if it was in the near future for women to stand up and be heard. Whether it was or not, Laura McBride would definitely be heard.

When she looked up into her husband's dark brown eyes, his soft look almost undid her. "What are you thinking, William?"

His eyes swept over her and she sensed the shift in his mood. He looked into her eyes and gave her a message that caused her heart to melt with joy. Pulling her close, he enfolded her in his arms and pressed his lips to hers.

As he deepened his kiss and ran his hand along her back, she melted into his arms. The message he was giving her was one of devotion and love.

Pulling back, he asked, "Do you want to go to the river and watch the sunset?"

Wanting to hear his romantic words once again, she said, "Describe a Mississippi sunset to me again."

He grinned as he said softly, "It's lovely and brings joy to my soul. You, my love, are like a Mississippi sunset to me."

Author's Notes

The inspiration for Laura's friend, Mary was my great, great grandmother, Martha Raymer Weaver. The governor kicked her family and 5000 others out of Missouri because they belonged to a church that did not believe in slavery: The Church of Jesus Christ of Latter-day Saints. The Missourians felt their beliefs would create a rebellion among the slaves so they needed to get rid of them. A few years later in Illinois, Martha was kicked out of her home by a Missouri mob once again and they burned it to the ground. I felt her experiences would add to this story, teaching us what prejudice can do to people.

Charles McGrath: He was an Irishman who pretended to be an itinerant Methodist preacher. While he conducted revival meetings, the Copeland Gang stole horses and slaves. They were a ruthless bunch of thieves, leaving violence and bloodshed wherever they went. In his camp meetings, McGrath preached, sang, prayed, and he even groaned as if possessed by the Holy Spirit. He begged his congregation to repent of their sins while his gang stole from them. Gale Wages, Charles McGrath, and James Copeland were the leaders of the gang and always dressed in disguise. That was why they were never caught. The gang consisted of sixty members and was active from 1830 to 1857.

Women Speaking in Public: In a pastoral letter from the Council of Congregationalist Ministers of Massachusetts, it said a woman who speaks publicly was "unwomanly and unchristian," saying that it would "threaten the female character with widespread and permanent injury."

Voting Rights for Women: Susan B. Anthony was arrested for voting illegally on November 5, 1872 in a presidential election. She was fined $100 but she refused to pay it. She said, *"Resistance to tyranny is obedience to God."*

The first four states to give women the right to vote were Wyoming (1890), Colorado (1893), Utah (1896), and Idaho (1896). It did not take long until women began running for office. (A note: Wyoming and Utah actually gave women the right to vote when they were just territories and weren't yet a state.)

The Female Relief Society was created in March of 1842 in Nauvoo, Illinois. The society was a mission of charity, giving relief to the distressed and needy. By March of 1844, the membership totaled 1331 women. The Female Relief Society is still giving service to this day and its headquarters is in Utah.

A Mississippi Sunset

Susan B. Anthony met with the Female Relief Society in Utah many times to discuss ways to spread the word of equality. More than 7.5 million women from The Church of Jesus Christ of Latter-day Saints belong to this organization.

Dancing Denounced: My daughter found a newspaper article when she was going through some old yellowed newspaper clippings that her grandmother had saved. There was no date or name of the newspaper, but this is what the clipping said: *The Reverend G. W. Simpson has uttered a strong denunciation of dancing in a letter to his parishioners. "Many think that there is very little harm in dancing, and I entirely agree. If only we had the right style of dancing; but, unfortunately, a style of dancing has been introduced into this country during comparatively recent times—I refer to the waltz and kindred dances—which in many cases cannot but excite the animal passions, and affords abundant opportunities for undue familiarity."*

The Abolition Movement: There were a lot of women who fought against slavery and gave lectures between 1821 – 1851.

Frederick Douglass, a man who had escaped servitude and was an abolitionist, wrote: "When the true history of the antislavery cause shall be written, women will occupy a large space in its pages; for the cause of the slave has been peculiarly a woman's cause." Douglass became a public speaker, author, and statesman.

The 1833 Meteor Shower: It lasted for nine hours. It frightened many people, making them believe the end of the world was at hand. In the Victorian Astronomy Writer, Agnes Clerke wrote:

"On the night of November 12 - 13, 1833, a tempest of falling stars broke over the Earth… The sky was scored in every direction with shining tracks and illuminated with majestic fireballs. At Boston, the frequency of meteors was estimated to be about half that of flakes of snow in an average snowstorm."

Baseball: In 1828, William Clarke published *The Boy's Own Book* that included the rules for baseball. Only underhand pitching was allowed. In 1845, the rules for baseball were changed to what we know today.

HISTORICAL ROMANCES

Willow Valley Historical Romances with a touch of mystery

One Last Dance: Felicity Brooks is a talented artist but her career is cut short when her father passes away. When Felicity meets their charming new neighbor, a fine-looking bachelor, she soon discovers that he is hiding his true identity. Nicholas Adams is on a quest. But that is not all. When she finds out that someone is after a valuable heirloom…a precious treasure that her father discovered in his attic, her life takes a new turn. After realizing how much she misses her father, will one last dance heal her broken heart?

Angel's Serenade: Emmeline Scott is raising her sister's two children and is surprised when she finds out the new doctor in town is helping her nephew adapt to his surroundings. Each day when Emmeline practices the piano, she doesn't know the doctor sits on the porch to listen to her music. As Emmeline gets to know the charming doctor, they become intrigued by her neighbor's mysterious behavior. Will they discover his secret? And who is the leader of the River Pirates, who is causing so much havoc?

A Pleasant Rivalry: Angelica Davis is surprised when she finds out that an old school chum has returned to Willow Valley to take over his grandfather's business. Since she writes articles for the Chronicle and Simon Morgan owns the Willow Valley News, they just happen to be rivals. The competition is on. Who will be the first to discover the identity of the jewel thief or the arsonist? Will it be Angelica or her rival? Gradually the old feelings she once had for Simon return as they both search for the same stories. To her surprise, Angelica realizes she is losing her heart to her rival.

Holidays in Willow Valley: A Collection of Six Holiday Stories: What were the holidays like at Willow Valley in 1840? How will Emmeline and Felicity celebrate Valentine's Day? Do Sam and Josie believe in leprechauns and the pot of gold when St. Patrick's Day comes around? Is it common to play jokes on one another on April Fools Day? Nicholas and Lucas find out first hand. Angelica's eyes are opened when she is challenged on Independence Day. When the Irish and Scottish came to America, they brought their Halloween traditions with them. How about Christmas? Will Willow Valley accept these traditions? Find out as you share their experiences. This book is full of surprises.

ABOUT AUTHOR

Linda Weaver Clarke was raised in the Rocky Mountains of Southern Idaho and now lives among the red desert hills of southern Utah. She is the author of Historical Romances, Swashbuckling/Adventure Romances, Romantic Cozy Mysteries, Mystery Suspense, a Children's Book, and Nonfiction.

Linda is a service missionary at the Family Search Center where she helps people find their ancestors so they can learn more about their heritage. She also teaches a class called Writing Your Family Legacy that is free to the public at the Family Search Center in St. George, Utah. To learn more, visit www.lindaweaverclarke.com.

Made in United States
North Haven, CT
10 June 2024